THE

ROSE

OF

NOTTINGHAM

Part of the Grim Nottingham series

By A. E. Johnson

Published by A E Johnson, Little Avalon,
Nottingham.
www.authoraejohnson.wordpress.com
contact cammbour@mail.com
Copyright © A E Johnson 2021
A E Johnson asserts the right to be identified as the
author of this work.

Books available from the Grim Nottingham Series
The Hangman's Turn
The Rose of Nottingham.

CHAPTER ONE LOST

I never expected it, never saw it coming. The signs were all there, but want clouded my eyes. Mother always used to say, 'You'll make a fine lady one day, Rose.' I was stupid enough to believe her. I remembered little of them, a faint smell of burnt embers always drew memories for me, of the days of happy, before it all went so wrong. My memories clouded, their faces hard to see, I know mother had dark hair, like me, always with large ringlets to the bottom, lips like bloodied roses, I looked a lot like her, not that I knew that now, mirrors were not something we kept in plenty at the workhouse.

My parents were not at fault for my future. They threw me into the muck after mother and father died. They were good people, hardworking, and not the type to be taken by illness or ailment. It all started with the Bloody Flux. When the shaking started, they took me from the house, 'twas the last I saw of mother and father. They had a pauper's funeral; when the house went back to the bank, they put me to work at Sutton workhouse in 1792. By 1802, I was one of the lucky ones. I left with my life intact, although sometimes, I regret that.

'Twas in my sixteenth year, sister Mary Evangeline always said I was a winter child, cold of the heart and fearing of none. I never quite knew what she meant. My aunt in Derby was a poor woman. She tried to take me on when my parents died, but she couldn't afford it. The sisters took care of all the unfortunate ones, including me, their Rose.

My education was normal. We would learn to darn, sewing, cooking, and cleaning, how to please a husband was on the top of our list, they missed out the part of how to get one. I always stood out in the workhouse. It was favourable to those who worked there, but those who resided there. They hated me, as a result they would punish me, and there was nothing they had left out. I had little by means of worldly possessions, all I had was my voice, head of the choir, they adored me in Sutton, each morning the people of the small village would gather outside to hear the heavenly nightingale sing, and I sang for them always, the words of God rang true from my voice, but my confession was simple, I attended church as any good Christian would; I prayed for the weak and needy, but I prayed to a wall and ceiling, God, if ever he were real, had left these lands many years ago, I struggled to believe in a being so mighty, he could not stop the beatings to a child, he could not end the poverty we so unfairly suffered, although my faith had failed me, something kept my hope alive, the hope that one day I would become a true lady, subservient to a worthy gentleman, someone to take care of me and I of him, someone to love me, and I him, someone to sing to, someone to hear my voice in my true self, not with words of God, but with the words of the real people.

As a child I had got hold of a newspaper. Within, I found several song sheets, pleasant words of hope and happiness. Those were the words I was longing to sing, and one day I would. Mr. Saunders, my voice, fascinated the groundskeeper of the workhouse, so much so he would bring me clippings of sheet music. He loved Handel and Mozart. I tried to learn them all by heart; I did not know what words I was singing, but I felt the music. I knew they were songs of love and anger, of calm and strife. He loved to hear me sing. I left Sutton as a lady, and when I hit the streets of Nottingham, I felt lost.

The way into Nottingham was frightening. The winding roads and looming trees terrified me, but they were nowhere near as frightening as the crowd when I arrived there. People pushing past to get the poorest cut of meat I'd seen in an age. Then there were the poor beggars, who seemed to swarm every corner. Before leaving Sutton, Mrs Huthwaite had me dressed, a flowing pink garment, frilled to the bottom and trimmed with a light pink lace. I looked like a proper lady in Nottingham. Even my hair was pretty to the back. I twirled tiny roses into the perfect plat. I was out of my depth; I know that now.

The first thing to hit me was the smell, the cold cobbles gave off a cold stench of dung from the animals at Beast Hill, the air was fresh that day as I passed through the Weekday Cross, a strong smell of fresh fish from the river was notable, but the noise would take some getting used to. Calling from every corner deafened me, all people trying to sell their wares. It was a noisy place, but I failed to see what I see now. The ladies upon street corners, the soft aroma of lavender drifted from all of them, a smell of strong pipe smoke hit me from the passing farm hands and masons toward the back of the Weekday.

I was hoping to find my way towards Fisher Gate. Sister Mary gave me letter to hand to a keeper when I arrived there. All I knew was Fisher Gate, and look for the brown door. The voice of Sister Mary would always comfort me. She was the sweet sister, unlike some others, who would gladly take turns to place a cane upon one's rear end for something as simple as slacking off. Sister Mary understood I was a lady, and I didn't want to let her down.

A lot of us leaving the Sutton Workhouse were lucky. Our overseers would always ensure we had somewhere to work for us when we arrived there. I could clean, but Mrs Huthwaite always warned me, 'Rose,' she would say, 'you may have a face as pretty as your name, but no good man of society wishes to hear you talking an ear off a donkey.' She was a wonderful woman, and her husband. I felt awkward to leave the workhouse, but my duty there ended. I now had a duty to myself. As God as my witness, I was a lady, and I could make a good wife for any man of good standing.

Fisher Gate was exactly that. My dress was the brightest thing on that street. I could feel the dirt cling to me as I made my way along the cold and muddy cobbles.

"Cleanliness is beside godliness," sister Mary would say. She ran a tight schedule in the workhouse, ensuring we were always pristinely clean was the first thing on her list.

Small baskets sprawled along the bottom of the buildings. Some still had a few of the crayfish in them, something I rarely saw in Sutton. Mr. Saunders treated us all once in the workhouse, bringing us a treat of crayfish.

The buildings were close together, barely enough space to fit a horse, but as I slowly made my way, looking at each door, I saw it, the brown door I was there to knock on. The two steps were green at the side. Moss had taken over them. Everything seemed damp in that place. I thought the workhouse was messy, 'twas nothing compared to this.

The door wasn't new either, a relic from the ark, a small brass doorhandle was all I could make out, the hour was creeping to late. I took a deep breath, accepting that this would be my fate. I would need to make a good impression. I straightened my dress, pulled up my small white gloves, and checked my hair was still neat.

Reaching forward, I went to knock, my hand disappeared straight through.

"Ark at you!" A plump redheaded lady stood at the door; my face must have been a picture of fright. "You must be Rose." Her glaring eyes inspected me.

"Yes, ma'am," I gave a curtsey, trying my way with proper manners.

"Ma'am," she scoffed, barging her way past me, carrying a bucket in each hand. "No one's called me ma'am in an age, even the old man ain't so..." She quickly turned, giving a scathing look. "You'll need to change, girl, can't be cutting fish looking like one of those flower girls from Harpers."

Her mocking of me was confusing. I thought I looked positively wonderful. Clearly, she did not agree.

"Can I ask what my duty will be?" I could feel my nerves deep in my stomach. I wasn't used to speaking with such rowdy people.

She invited me in. The house was pleasant enough, nothing a good clean couldn't fix.

"Ya skin 'em, gut 'em, cut 'em and bone 'em," she abruptly hurried, she quickly turned, facing me she gave a deathly stare. "You worked before?"

"I was in the Sutton Workhouse, so, I did a few things, Ma'am."

"The name is Gladys," she raised her brows, showing the deep stress lines on her forehead; she wiped her wet hands on her dirty cotton pinafore. "Come on, I'll show ya." She gave a tight smile. I could see she was a friendly woman, abrupt, rowdy, and overly excitable, but friendly.

Following her to the back of the small house, a stench hit me. The indescribable smell of fish filled my lungs. I would smell of the creatures for months following. I never remembered such an unpleasant smell. They gave fish to us at Sutton in batches of soups and stews. I had rarely experienced it so fresh before.

Stepping outside, a small courtyard met us. Looming brick walls sheltered us from those lingering within the alleyways. Smoke from the chimneys bellowed a thick black mist into the skies. A large man stood at a table. A large pinafore wrapped around him, covered with the guts of the creatures on his table.

"Watch our Tom here," said Gladys. She stood at the side of him, inviting me to join her. He looked at me, giving a tight smile through his thick brown beard.

His hand swung back, slamming into the table. The head of a fish flew across the yard, a spray of blood flew toward me. It ruined my ladies' dress, and I would forever be a fishmonger's apprentice.

I watched Tom close; he taught me all I needed to know of cutting and gutting. It was an unpleasant duty, but it would be my duty until I found a husband of my own. I was proud of the new skills I had learnt in such little time; I was no expert in the matter of killing fish, but I certainly knew a thing or two about the fundamentals in fish gutting, certainly not something a gentleman would wish to hear of, but it brought a small wage, a roof over my head, and a future.

The docks toward the Leen would take the boats onto the Trent, some days, large boats would make their way up the large river, carrying sea fish, they weren't the freshest, and so we would have to be quick to get them to market. Taking the tables along Fisher Gate to get them straight to the Weekday was at first a daunting task, but eventually my duty eased. As the days passed, my hands hardened, and so did my spirit.

Gladys was a wonderful host. I had my own room within the home of Gladys and Thomas Cartwright, a larger space than I knew before. My chambers were enough for a single lady. They even provided a sort of uniform, a long brown skirt, and a light brown shirt with a tailored waistcoat. Of course, I would usually have my bloodstained pinafore.

For the first few weeks, life was good, 'twas a welcome change from the Workhouse. At sixteen, I was ready to search for the gentleman to make a genuine lady of me. Each day I would journey toward the Weekday Cross, 'twas a short distance from Fisher Gate. The walk past the Gaol always frightened me. Hearing those poor souls calling from inside chilled me each time. Every gent who passed received a smile from me. I did not want to make myself seem like an easy target, but I needed to make them question my availability.

The Weekday offered Gladys a place to sell her goods; we had a large fish stand within the Weekday, I would deliver each day to the stall, but not before delivering Mr. Stafford his vinegared cockles. He was a character. He would spend the day wandering the town, selling off his potted cockles. He made a living for him and his wife.

The Weekday Cross gave me a chance to see all the eligible bachelors of the town. However, there were few for a lady of my age. Passing back towards Fisher Gate, a well-dressed gentleman ambled towards me. I knew his face but struggled to place him.

He pulled his hat down to greet me, "Ma'am," he wore a struggling smile upon his aging face.

I curtsied, "Sir," I said. Politeness was the way of any lady. "Do I know you, Sir, you are awfully familiar."

He seemed stricken by my words, as though no one had spoken to him in an age. "Francis, Ma'am, Francis Monrow," he shook his aging face, unable to place me. "Town magistrate." Stepping back, I was awfully pleased. He was a fine gentleman in town. I was but a child to him. "I recognise your face, Ma'am. Have you been in Nottingham long?"

His question unnerved me. Somehow, I knew this man, but I did not know how. "No, sir, I arrived but a week ago."

"May I ask where from?"

"From Sutton, Sir," I could not say the name. Workhouse children carried a poor reputation. I did not want the judge to think of me as a pauper.

"Sutton," he gave a pondering look. "Well, I hope to see you around more often. The town can always use more beauty."

I was bashful. Slowly, I walked away. "I live with a family on Fisher Gate. I am the apprentice to a fishmonger's wife, but I plan on changing my vocation, as soon as something is available."

"Or someone perhaps," he gave a downward smile. I knew his thinking. "If I were thirty years younger, your vocation would change in an instant, my dear."

I gave a bashful laugh. I knew I looked older for my age, but the sixty something judge was attempting to woo a sixteen-year-old. I felt unnerved, but I still recognised his face.

Passing back towards Fisher Gate, something felt strange. I knew I was being watched on the busy street, but something felt stronger than a simple watch, something much more lingering followed me. The house was empty upon my return. Tom was out on the river. He wouldn't return until late that evening.

The morrow would bring an early start to the day, and so I began readying supper for the return of Gladys. Placing some stew on the boil, I made my way towards the well out back. The cold air felt fresh upon my skin, the feeling remained. A small wall toward the back of the courtyard hid the back of the house from the alleyway.

Washing my face, I heard the screeching of a cat, shocked; I looked up, that feeling became stronger.

I found bravery, "Who's there?" I called out, but no one replied. I began again washing the day away from my skin, and then I felt it.

Taken from behind, a hand covered my mouth, two enormous arms caught my hands, dragging me back inside the house I tried to scream, I tried to kick, I tried everything, but nothing seemed to get the brute off me. Throwing me to the floor, I hit my head on the cold flagstone floor. A stench of ale came with each breath towards me. I could feel him clambering onto the back of me as I lay helpless on the floor.

He tangled his fingers in my hair, forcing my head to the floor. I did not know it hurt that much. I was a lady; I had never felt something so awful. He held my neck as he forced me to do the one thing I had saved for my future husband. I glared toward the bottom of the poorly painted kitchen cupboard, I felt it all, but I did not move, I failed to scream or call out, I felt him, every bit of his feral skin pressing on mine, the drips of filthy sweat landing on the nape of my neck, the pain was but a whisper of the pain I felt deep in my soul.

I was a lady, but no one would want me now. As damaged goods, like the fish from the sea we would throw to the gulls, no one would want me, especially not a gentleman. I was going to be a lady, and now, I was nothing.

I never expected it. When Gladys returned, I sat at the old wooden kitchen table. I could not even remember pulling myself from the ground; my arms wrapped around me, I could still feel him on me.

"What happened to you?" she hurried towards me; noticing the cut on the front of my head.

"I was... something happened." I couldn't stop the tears. Gladys held onto me. She got a cloth and put it on my cut. The pain made me wince, but there was another pain, one she couldn't see.

"Rose, what happened?"

Her shivering voice worried me. We had grown rather close, and I didn't wish to upset her.

"I tried to fight him off, but he was too strong," my voice became too high for her to hear.

"Rose, did he?" I could hear she was awkward. All I had to do was look at her. She knew I couldn't bring myself to say it, but she knew.

That night, I had no appetite, I kept thinking about him, I didn't know what he looked like, all I needed to do was turn and I would've seen him, I could hardly remember anything after having my head hit into the floor.

Mr. Cartwright soon came home. We would usually have retired, but Gladys insisted we stay up. I could hear them in the other room. They were talking about me, about what he did.

"Well, if she's attracting those sorts, we can't have her here." His cruel words shook me and forced a hearty punch from Gladys.

"I'll hear no such thing. That could've been me, could've been anyone." She did not hide her words, she no longer spoke in hushed tones. "We need to tell the law, they should pass later, keep your eyes on the street or make your way to the gaol. 'Tis our duty to the girl at only sixteen to ensure her safety, and we have failed her."

"What do you expect of me?" he moaned. His callousness was no surprise. He was a busy man. "I ain't her dad, Gladys, and you ain't her mother, she's a grown girl. Things like this 'appen, they ain't nice but they 'appen."

"I could bloody clout you right now. They only 'appen in places as run down as this."

"Oh, so this is my fault now, not having a trade to keep us away from the scum of mongers, well you married into it, Gladys, you were fine then, why the sudden change?"

"We should have our trade regardless, without the fear of our apprentice being felt up by some stranger..."

"That was more than a feeling up..." his mocking forced me to stand. I could hear no more of their arguing.

"Thomas Gregory Cartwright, you watch your tongue. That girl is fixing herself to be a lady, but what now, he ain't just taken her innocence, he's taken her future."

"I truly apologise for the inconvenience I've caused you." I stood by the door. I could feel myself shaking. They both turned to see me. Their heated arguing died. "I was rather excited to be a lady, and I believe I still can be, but I don't believe I can do that here, I've clearly caused you hassle, and I don't mean to do that either, I can return to Sutton on the morrow."

"No," Gladys softly said, stepping towards me. I could see a pain in her eyes. "I failed to be a mother, but I will never fail at being a guardian, you're staying, we'll get him, and he will find his end on George's rope."

Her promise remained with me that night, I could hardly find sleep, each time my eyes closed I remembered a little more, the pain, the breath upon my neck, even the way he held my neck at the back, but I remembered in my dreams, I could feel a cold sharp steel pressed against my neck. I woke with gasps of breath each time I remembered more. Their whispers had also kept me questioning most of the night, the walls were thin enough to hear Gladys and Tom talking, their muffled voices did not sound concerned, they sounded odd, as though what happened was normal to them, 'twas not normal to live in the company of monsters.

The morning came, and it was cold, the spring on the river was usually bright and pleasing to the eye, but 'twas grey and dull. The morning chorus seemed to sympathise with me. The birds remained silent. Sat by my window, I saw no one upon the streets outside.

'Two men came with a bale of hay, chasing the rabbits and crows away, five men came with a horse for two, trample the flowering morn of dew, hark now horse you'll change thine mood, the farmers bring you fresh winter food.'

'Twas a favourite of mine. It calmed me, but I still struggled to understand what the song was all about. I often thought of writing my own, but I had minor talent by ways of writing.

CHAPTER TWO ON THE MORROW

The house was cold that morning. A strange dullness lingered in the stagnant dust which floated about my room. I had little sleep, but I would need to be at the Weekday in time to deliver to Gladys. A day had passed since the beast had violated me. I had refused to leave that day, choosing to remain in the shadows of the gloomy house. I spent the day cleaning, so much so my hands now bled from the scrubbing years of grime from the walls.

Making my way down the stairs, I could hear muffled voices. No one should've been in the house that morning. I felt a cold shiver up my spine; I remained on the stairs listening to the voices in the living room which the stairs led straight towards. The front door was at the bottom of the stairs. I could run, but I didn't know if they locked the door or not.

"I'll go get her," 'twas the voice of Gladys I was hearing.

"Be quick," the man with her demanded. He sounded callous. What happened to me had happened to so many others. He cared not for the consequences of what it had done to workhouse scum.

She came to the bottom of the stairs. Peering up, she could see I was already there, looking guilty on the stairs.

"It's alright, it's the law, a man called Godfrey, said he can help."

I was reluctant at first. Step by step, I felt my feet grow heavy coming down the stairs. The man looked kind, he looked forgiving, but he seemed to look straight through me.

"Rose, glad to see you're well." He was a handsome chap, a well-dressed sheriff's man. He even removed his hat and stood to greet me.

"I might look well, but I can assure you, Sir, I'm far from it." I still felt ill, sleeplessness, and a pain in my head still hindered me.

The man, Godfrey, turned to Tom. "Has she seen the physician?" Tom shook his head. He looked ashamed. I know if he were there, he would've protected me. He was a good man, simple, but kind.

"We have no need for a physician," blurted Gladys, rushing towards me as she held me by the shoulders. "This girl has been through the worst day of her life..."

"She's an apprentice, from a workhouse. I mean no disrespect, but I've seen inside of those places. I doubt this was the worst thing to happen to her..."

"Hold ya tongue," I spat. I could feel my blood run white hot. I could barely look at the man. A sickness gripped me. "No one ever did that in Sutton. They were kind, gentlefolk, but if this is how you run your streets, I will speak to Francis Monrow." His head lifted; he knew the name well. "Yeah, I know him. We get on quite well, and I bet he would love to hear of your misconduct."

"Ma'am, I mean no offence..."

"Too late." I marched my way toward the flowered sofa. Years of grime covered the material, but I still sat as a lady in a parlour. "I remember very little, but what I know, is there is a man out there taking something no one can get back, look to him as a thief, that way you'll probably find him."

"We will do all we can. Do you know what he looked like?"

"Dark hair, I know he had dark hair, because the hair on his arms was dark," I felt my eyes drift to the black smear to the top of the fireplace, I tried to remember, but every time I did, something blocked it, forcing my mind to stop. "I remember... I was in the back, but I think he watched me, coming up Fisher Gate. I could feel his eyes."

"Did you see anyone in Fisher Gate? anyone who isn't usually there?"

I shook my head. I didn't know what he wanted me to do. I was trying to relive it, but it took so much from me.

"Well, get her to the physician, her injuries are minor, but it would be worth a check."

Oh, that word, minor, minor injuries. I could've ripped his heart out. They weren't minor injuries.

"I hope you never have children, Sir," I stood to face him. "I was to be a lady, he took that from me, I was to be a good wife, he took that as well, I was to be a good woman, faithful to god, he took that too, he took my future, my everything. You may see this as minor, but a workhouse did not raise me, 'twas good women of God, by a man who understood the sanctity of god, the delicateness of a lady, and he taught me that, it is nothing minor to have your future ripped from you by a hungry animal in the night. If ever you have a daughter, I hope this never happens to her, because then you'll see, these ain't no minor injuries, he took my life, Sir, and all I ask, is that you find him and make him suffer, make him suffer as I will suffer for the rest of my days, no one may take that from someone, 'tis something one should give, never take."

I moved him almost to tears. He lowered his head as he made his way out of the door. I didn't think he would find him, but I just hoped he would try.

The days passed like a cold flash. I set my routine, and I couldn't remember the last time I smiled. I was nothing but an apprentice, at sixteen, I was eligible to care for myself, but Gladys and Tom did all they could for me, I became like a daughter to them, they even took me to the physician, and paid for my medication to help with the pain and night terrors. Many would pass me off as fit for the new asylum, but they did not give up on me. They persisted with my nightmares, sharing them with me, comforting me through.

The weeks soon passed, the pain in my head disappeared, nothing but a small scar sullied my face, but Gladys still got me my weekly laudanum. It helped mostly at night, letting me drift into a dreamless sleep.

The only thing that helped was my voice, the quaint little songs I had heard from the village pub in Sutton being sang on a drunken evening, I would sing them to my new audience, to Gladys and Tom, 'twas the only time I were happy.

"You'll make a wonderful entertainer one day. If only this were London, they would have snatched you up by now." Gladys sat beside the open fire darning socks, a task she found ever so relaxing, one I found utterly boring.

"Well, if I could find a stage, my life would be complete," I mocked. I knew I would never make it to stage. No one wanted to listen to a workhouse brat harping on about cloudy weather.

"I'm sure any would take you." A compliment from Tom was certainly not what I was expecting.

"You'll go places, my dear. I see it now, Rose," Gladys smiled towards me. I could not see it, how I could ever use my voice as a vocation.

"We'll see, but I enjoy it here though, with a proper family." I felt like they were becoming a family to me, the clothes they had given me, even the dingy room I had to myself. I felt at home there, because of who I shared it with.

Walking down that street got harder. Every day I would spend a little extra time along High Pavement, not wanting to walk that street, feeling those eyes constantly on me. The feeling only got worse.

The morning I remember it all changed, I woke to a thought. I would always have to walk that street. I was brave for going on as long as I did, but my bravery came from my tincture.

Stood at the front door, I held my boxes ready to take to Gladys who would already be at the Weekday. Tom had left early that morning. The boats on the river wouldn't be back until late. I felt myself freeze; I didn't want to be in that house, but the street was more terrifying than ever. His eyes were still on me. I tried to put my foot on the step, but it wouldn't move.

Muffled calling and echoes in the streets unnerved me more. I felt my hands shake, dropping the boxes to the steps. I was lucky they did not break. Rushing into the house, I reached into the kitchen cupboard for my bottle. A quick straw calmed me, just enough to see me from the house.

The dark street greeted me. Everything seemed dark now. A blackness to the town had taken over. I longed to see those bright days of summer again, like in Sutton. When the daffodils would line the bottom of the house, crocus and lily would shoot through roughly trimmed grasses. It was a far throw from the world I knew.

Nottingham was not what they promised me. The stench of the streets clung to my skin, a smell of industry, smoke bellowed from the large buildings along Lace Market, I did not know their business there, even the crystal waters of the Leen were brown, what should've been an abundance of fish was missing there, the Trent also had a smell to it, of rotting vegetation and the depressive stench of dead things, the banks filled with a thick black mud, the cold weather would bring a steam from the surface of the water, stinking the town out.

Mrs. Lily was a housekeeper at the workhouse, they gave her the duty in the kitchens, making sure we shared our rations correctly, she always used to say, 'The sun will always shine upon smiling faces,' my sun dulled and left me now, I struggled to remember the last time I smiled, or the last time I was even glad.

High Pavement was busy that morn. I remained with Gladys for a while at the stall, not wanting to return just yet. The day's duty would be very little anyway, given that the boats with the fish wouldn't be arriving until noon. It offered a busy day on the morrow.

"You need to get yer head together, Rose," Gladys busily said. Serving customers as they passed seemed to be a talent of hers. I struggled with even one. "What happened, it was shockingly awful, and I'll never make light the act, but it happened. Ya need to deal with it. Move on." Passing the last customer a wrapped carp, she spun. "Now, do you wish to spend your life as an apprentice, or would ya rather make yersen a proper fishwife?"

"Well, neither, really. I always rather dreamed of having a husband who worked in industry, a man of excellent reputation, respectable, like a magistrate."

She cast a look of shocked doubt. "Eh, don't we all, love. Anyway, the boats won't be back until later, but Harry will be by the house soon with some cockles to boil and pack. It's alright, love, you can trust Harry, he's a lout but a good one, too old to make you a husband but he could have a son or two knocking round knowing him."

Fisher Gate was cold, empty. Passing Bridge Foot, I felt a strange feeling. I was collecting some of the old buckets we would all use, ready for when Harry arrived. I was quick with my task. Rushing back up Fisher Gate a sudden feeling of fear spilt into me, my blood ran cold, the hairs of my skin stood on end, I struggled with the front door, trying desperately to get in, the old, rusted lock wouldn't open.

I screamed, feeling a large hand on my shoulder I quickly turned, the man stood back. "Ya alreet, love, I'm not gonna harm ya."

He held his hands up, showing me he meant no harm. I wiped my tears away, looking to the ground he had four large sacks with him. Wet sand covered the bottom of the sacks.

"Are you Harry?"

He lifted his hat, holding it to his chest, "Ma'am, I never meant te frighten ya, just come for a delivery is all."

"Thank you," I opened the door with ease, 'twas strange I struggled so hard with it. I invited Harry in, knowing he would need to carry the sacks to the backyard for me to prepare.

"Seems like you've had quite a fright, young un." He carried them to the back, placing them at the back door. "A young girl like you, shouldn't be alone in a place such as Nottingham town."

"What makes you say that?" I felt my lip quivering, not knowing what his reply would be.

"Well, word has it to be on the lookout for a man doing harm te young uns, like you, keep the doors locked, Tom and Gladys will take care of ya, but when they ain't ere, ya got to keep yersen safe, now, as soon as I'm gone, you lock them doors, ya arkin?"

"Yes." I couldn't hold it. I needed it, my little bottle of help. I turned to the cupboard behind me, reaching for my tincture.

"Tut, tut, tut," he slowly shook his head, "a young un like you shouldn't need such vices, get rid a that stuff, while ya mind is still yer own."

I looked at the bottle. It seemed harmless enough. It simply helped me forget that night. It made me confident. It made me a lady. I was a lady when I had my confidence and my pride. The laudanum made sure of it.

As soon as Harry left, I locked the door. We had a large pit in the yard we would use for boiling the water, so the house didn't stink of fish on an evening. I got the heavy black pots and boiled the poor creatures. The spitting shells as they boiled in the pots were mesmerising. I hardly noticed how dark it was getting. Gathering clouds darkened it more.

Hearing the door to the front open, I made my way in. Gladys had just arrived back, 'twas a hard day on the market, I could tell, given the redness to her face. I set some of the fish pie down I made for her. She smiled at me, but it wasn't a normal smile. I imagined if I had a mum, that's how she would look at me. I wanted to make Gladys and Tom proud, I wanted to make them like me, but, I didn't wish to stay as a fishmonger's apprentice, or as a fishwife, I was a lady, and I wanted to find a gentleman who could prove that to the world and all.

"I smell you've got the cockles going?"

"I did. As soon as Harry came, he gave me a fright when he first turned up." I was in a lighter mood. Having Gladys back made me feel safer. "He said though, that my tincture, it isn't good for me, why would he say that?"

I asked an innocent question, or at least I thought it was. She didn't seem pleased by my questioning. "Never you mind what Harry says, don't it make ya feel better?"

"It does." I pushed the kettle to the fire, starting a brew.

"Then if it helps, it helps, you're a good one, Rose, don't let opinions of others melt you, you're a good girl. Now keep being a good girl and be sure to listen to me an Tom."

"Of course I will," I looked toward the back door. The cockles were steaming. They would about be ready for the next lot. "You taught me a lot, and I'll never let that go. If it helps, it helps, and if you think I need it, I have every reason to trust you."

"Yes you do, now, to the cockles, before the' boil over."

Running out I moved them off the boil, putting the next lot in, I shook them over the cool water, I knew this process now, 'twas something I never thought of, even when Mr. O'Riley, the groundskeeper at Sutton, would treat us all to cockles, I never thought of the work involved. If only he could see me now, I was doing Sutton proud.

Wandering back into the house, I reached for my tincture, knowing I would need a little boost before bed.

"How did you and Tom meet?" I sat at the table, my eyes were heavy, it was fast that tincture.

"I was the daughter of a fisherman. His mam was a fishwife as well. We met through trade. We stick together, us on Fisher Gate. We keep it close." I heard a scream from the street, breaking the trance I felt. "Sit, never ya mind that, just the girls' next door."

"Someone could hurt them." I worried about those girls she spoke of. Just like I did, they needed help.

"They welcome it, love, we have four brothels on this street alone, probably the reason they ain't caught the fiend who had you yet."

I felt my heart sink, a sickening grip in my stomach of torturous loss. "I didn't know those places were here. Why didn't you say?"

"What good would it do, love?" she was callous. She cared not for what happened to me that night. "Worry not, you're getting better by the day, keep at your tincture, you'll be well on the morrow."

I drifted back into my chair, I couldn't believe we lived in such a place, no wonder I always had a feeling of being watched, those filthy men watching where I was going, what I was doing, if I were available to them, and then the women, those soulless women, who sell themselves further from a good and pure life, I was a good girl, I would never fall for such things.

The morning darkened the day; I sorted my cockles, but a strange smell lingered as I stepped out. I checked to be sure the fire was out, but I could still smell burning, a smoke lingered in the air, a smell of burnt wood was thick. Looming clouds above made me realise 'twas not my fire causing the problems. I stepped onto Fisher Gate. I had to go back in. Taking my tincture, I took the bottle, sliding it into my pinafore. I would need the cart that day. Taking the vinegared cockles was a heavy task. I would need my bottle of strength with me.

Wandering past the houses on Fisher Gate, I glanced to each window, I could see them inside, a small woman, a red wrap around her shoulders stood at the door of one of the houses, her look towards me told me she knew, my extended knowledge had hit her. The Weekday was quiet, only a few wandering about.

"Cockles," I was out of breath arriving at the stall, Gladys laughed at the sight of me, "you're looking to be better this morn."

"I'm feeling more hopeful."

"That's what I like ta hear, and your bottle will help with that." She looked at my pinafore. "I see you have your bottle of confidence, well if that's what you need, then so be it. Now, back to the house with ya."

Walking back, I took the long way, going through Brightmore Hill and onto Narrow Marsh. The streets were busier there, the speeding carts coming towards me, swirling voices

in the air, strange sounds of laughter coming from
the building beside me, it all seemed so close,
they were laughing in my ear, the carts and horses
were too close to me, everything spun around
me, I couldn't breathe, I couldn't focus, nothing
made sense. I shot into an alley to the side. The
closing walls of the houses were crushing.
Reaching for my tincture, I felt my body relax the
second it hit my tongue.

This was no normal way for a lady to be.
I knew I needed to get back to Fisher Gate. I
knew I needed to just get in the house and
Gladys would be right. I would be fine come the
morrow.

CHAPTER THREE NO TIME LIKE THE NOW

The afternoon brought a heavy rain that day. I could feel a bitterness in the air. The smell along Narrow Marsh gave off a scent of fresh grasses. New buildings were springing up daily, a tension was in the air through the Lace Market, I could feel an anger brewing, the Luddites of the mills were unhappy with the loss of jobs, winter was far-reaching yet, but it seemed to hit quicker, knowing we came towards a winter of hardship.

"I could always get different work." I helped Gladys in the kitchen, I say helped, she sat at the table and watched me as I cleaned the greying walls from years of dirt and grime. "I mean, I could still be an apprentice for you, but you know yourself, the river doesn't give good during winter."

"We've survived before, we'll survive again, the winter is harsh but it's fair."

"Even with a grain shortage?" asked Tom. His thunderous frame stepped into the kitchen, blocking the small archway toward the parlour.

"Even with a shortage," Gladys replied. I could hear the worry in her voice, but I knew we would get through it as a family.

"The girl is right, she may need other work through the winter, now is the time to be looking, those pouring out of St Peters this morning looked worried, I know the priest likes to make 'em panic, but even George worries."

"George Smith?" asked Gladys.

I turned to listen to the conversation. "He said those of the river need to find something now. He don't want mongers on his gallows."

"Gallows?" I worried, not knowing what Tom meant.

"He's a good man, our George, knows what he's talking about. He worries for us, and with good reason."

"What reason?"

"He said the church won't have enough funds to help everyone, so as I say it's best Rose finds work now, at least she can keep hersen through winter that way, besides, with your voice you won't struggle, plenty of places in the town want to hear a pretty sound, look to a pretty face, all with eligible gentlemen waiting."

I saw Tom roll his eyes; he doubted my dream of becoming a lady. Gladys looked towards me, not knowing what to say. She liked me, I could feel it.

"I promise that I'll still stay. I'll do all I can, to get good work for us all."

"You're a good girl, Rose. Perhaps that dream of yours of having a gentleman one day, it ain't so farfetched after all."

The morning brought a strange light, a dullness took over as the daunting winter approached. The morning was still dark as I made my way into town. I wouldn't know where to find work. Neither did Tom nor Gladys. They had grown among the fishermen. I would begin my search on High Pavement. Sometimes they would pin jobs at the side of the Gaol near the county house. I was hoping to find something there.

Passing Bridge Foot, I had a feeling I was being followed; I looked down, trying to peep behind me, sure enough there she was, the woman from a few doors down, she followed every step I made, a red shawl draped around her small pale arms, long black gloves reached past her elbows, a large black hat with red trim along the top. I quickened my pace, not knowing what mischief she brought.

"Rose," she called out to me. I felt a bolt hit me. I don't know how she knew my name. "Rose, please wait, you shouldn't be out in this darkness."

She spoke with a good tongue. She sounded to be from good breeding. I slowed, looking to the cobbled streets. The bells of St Peters called out. I kept my eyes down.

"Rose, you can stand straight. I don't mean you any mischief or harm, just a lady taking a lady towards town," her soft voice enticed me. She seemed kind.

"I apologise, you never know who's about." I gave a false laugh. I think she could tell. She looked down, seeing my tincture in the pocket of my dark blue dress. I quickly covered it with my hand.

"What has you out, anyway? I thought Tom was taking the deliveries from now on?"

"He is. I'm on the search for work." She seemed so nice. She walked beside me, making sure I was safe getting into town. She was older than me, a lot older, looked to be in her thirties. "You wouldn't know of any employ, would you?"

"For a lady like you, nothing, the flower shops are still open, but they close a lot this time of year, I know the knitters are not having much luck, since the Luddites started, 'twould be best you avoid that area my dear."

"Well, do you know anywhere?" I was desperate, I wanted to make Gladys proud, and Tom, they had been so good to me, taking me in as an apprentice, even paying for my tincture.

"I know of a few places my dear, but a girl as pure as you, nothing, sorry." Her raven hair perfectly platted and curled to the back of her. A few wisps fell to the front of her face. She was beautiful.

"If you know of something, anything, please let me know."

"Of course I will."

"But how did you know? How did you know Tom would deliver from now on?" I felt a strange suspicion grow, an uneasy feeling of mistrust.

She had a derisive tone, "Rose, like you, I'm a lady, 'tis my duty to know the business of my street, but also, the walls are paper thin, I hear all from my abode, why not visit some time, and see for yourself." Her lips moving were odd. She spoke, but her lips seemed to linger. They swelled red.

"I might do, but first, I need to find work."

"Just stay away from the Lion, they're always looking for sweet young girls." She had no reason to worry about me, she had no loyalty to me. It made me wonder why she was being so kind. "Just a warning, Rose. Be careful who you trust. Every Rose has thorns."

I watched as she left, making her way towards Drury Hill. I wondered what she meant by 'Girls as pure as me.' I carried on towards the Gaol, I saw a large man, smartly dressed, pass into the Gaol.

Looking to the notice boards, all I could see were notices of the cease letters of the Luddites. They had caused some awful issues in the town. They had turned whole buildings into rubble due to them. I glared at that board for ages, but I could see nothing.

Just as I gave up, I turned to make my way back, and there he was, Judge Francis Monrow, I curtsied as I saw him, he tilted his hat, I liked the way he dressed, 'twas an older style he liked, knee breeches and brass buttons, just like Thomas Bayley, who would preach in the church in Sutton.

"Morning, your honour."

"Oh, your honour now," he mocked. I didn't know how else to address him. He was a judge. "I hope you're well." He narrowed his eyes, looking into mine. "I see a greying around your eyes, are you sleeping well?"

"Not so much, Sir, we hear a heavy winter is heading towards us, the fishing trade isn't the best in winter, so I thought it best I find a job now, to better provide for those who took me on as an apprentice in the first place, so I can care for them through the hard months."

"Such a caring young girl." He held a wide smile towards me. I could tell he liked me. I only hoped he could help. "I tell you what, on the early morrow make your way towards Goose Gate, there is a building on the corner of Goose Gate and Broad Lane, make your way in the back entrance, never the front, ask to speak to a man named John Bentley, he will direct you to a place of employ."

I felt my heart race, pattering on my chest, "Thank you, a thousand times, thank you." I could've cried for the judge and his generosity.

"No need. A beautiful lady deserves the best access to life. As I say, only use the back door on Goose Gate."

I frantically nodded, "I will, Sir, thank you again."

He tilted his hat and made his way up the steps of the Gaol. Rushing back to Fisher Gate, I could barely hold my excitement. Cutting down Short Hill, I rushed as fast as I could, holding my heavy dress as I did.

Gladys would be so pleased to hear the news. My excitement carried me back upon a cloud. Reaching the end of Fisher Gate, there she stood again. The lady with the red shawl seemed to wait for me on the doorstep.

"You seem rather pleased; did you find what you were looking for?"

I couldn't contain my smile. "I did, miss, a wonderful chance."

"May I ask where?" her inquisitive eyes softened towards me, almost flirting.

"A place on the corner of Goose Gate and Broad Lane, Judge Francis Monrow himself invited me there." I was overly excited, but I saw her smile wither.

"What has you so hooked on finding employ, girl?"

"I need it, the winter won't be kind."

"Well, just you be careful," her smile had faded to a frown, her rose-red lips seemed to spill fear and torture, "that place isn't all it seems, Rose, it's not meant for young ones like you, it certainly isn't a place for a lady, and by the grace of god do not let them hear you sing."

"The judge himself pointed me there. A man of such esteem wouldn't do such a thing unless it was with good intention..."

"Or money. I wouldn't trust a judge, Rose." I felt my skin itch on my arm, a cramp in my stomach forced me forward, I felt sick, a sudden dark cloud seemed to fall upon me. "You alright, Rose?" she came down from the step.

"I'm alright, mmm, excited, sall," I could feel my eyes flickering, my tongue wouldn't work right, I could barely get my words out.

"Take it girl, I know you need it." She looked at my pocket where I kept my bottle. Reaching for it, I came to the side, away from prying eyes. I had hardly any left, and I knew Gladys wouldn't be back for a while with more from Mr. Carr, who had a chemist on Long Row.

She could see my struggle. My hands were shaking. I could barely hold the bottle. "Why don't you come in, Rose, you'll find everything you'll ever need in here."

"Perhaps later," I lost my thought, "I don't even know your name."

"The name is Cynthia, we're all friends here, Rose. I can get you what you need."

Her chastened look forced my eyes shut. I tried to gain focus. "As I say, perhaps later."

"Come on, Rose, ain't no time like the now."

"Oi!" I heard Gladys calling up Fisher Gate, rushing towards me. "Clear off."

"Oh, come on, Gladys," she folded her arms and leant back on the dirty brick wall behind her, rolling her eyes, "I don't need an apprentice, you know that."

She seemed to anger Gladys, her very presence unhinged her. "She has no interest in your, ways," she spat.

"Oh, Gladys, I would never move in on your property," Cynthia leant towards me, "She tell you, did she? How many apprentices she's had before you?" Her raised brows forced me to question. I turned to Gladys, lowering my brow.

"They were different, all girls who found their way in the town, but you're with us now, and that's how it'll be," she turned to Cynthia, "You keep your nose out of our business." Her threat was apparent. Cynthia held her hands up. She made her way up the dirty steps and back into the darkness of the house.

"Don't you be listening to a word she has to say, you keep away from that house." She took my shoulder, forcing me back toward the house, handing my bottle to me as an instant relief fell over me. I wondered what Gladys was talking about, and I also wondered what Cynthia meant by the amount of apprentices she'd had, but I didn't question further, I kept going, heading into the house and I could finally drift off to my pain-free world with my tincture.

The morrow was a bright morning. I dressed as beautifully as I could, wearing the pink trim dress I'd arrived in. Gladys did a wonderful job of getting the stains out. That walk towards Goose Gate had me nervous, each step along the cold cobbles made me trip and lose balance, I was lucky I had brought a small purse, enough to get my bottle in, I kept pulling to the side, just for a quick drop.

Arriving at Goose Gate, I saw the building. I stood at the front door, but I knew not to go in. Two stone lion heads looked toward me on the lonely pavement. I walked along, just a short way to see a small brown door. I gave a small knock, not wanting to startle those inside.

The creaking door opened to a well-dressed young gent. He looked young, early twenties, and handsome, very handsome, dressed in a black suit with red and gold trim. He looked ready for a day of business.

"Sir," I curtsied, "Judge Monrow sent me, to see a man called John Bentley."

His smile brightened his face. He looked me up and down as I stood uncomfortably on the pavement. "Turn around," he did not ask, he commanded. I thought it frightfully odd, but I turned. "You'll do just fine," he opened the door wide.

"Thank you, Sir, may I ask what business this is?"

"'Tis a gentleman's club," he replied. He quickly took me through the dark, winding hall. We came to a large room, a circular bar was in the middle. Toward the back of the bar, a long staircase led to a balcony, beneath which a large round stage was situated. I felt a strange feeling of belonging there. "Worry not, we will give you all the training needed to fulfil your role to perfection."

He walked fast, past the bar and the round tables. It looked like a place fit for kings, a place where I would find true gentlemen. There was a smell of smoke, mingled with an aromatic scent of men's cologne, the type of fancy stuff they got from the chemist.

"I'll take you to the room you'll be using."

"May I ask my purpose here?" I worried, I don't know why, but looking back, I realise now, the dark wood of the banister, plush red leather on the chairs, it was a gentleman's club, but I didn't really know what gentlemen were like, I had met few in my time.

"Your duty, if I give you the position, will be companionship, your addiction will help," he looked at my purse. "Come on, girl, it sticks out like a negro in a crowd, you would do better to cover it."

"It's for pain, Sir."

"Pain." His sniggering made me feel so low. "Use whatever excuse you wish, just remember, to you 'tis an addiction, to those you will entertain, 'tis nothing but a habit, the gentlemen here have every need to indulge in the escape provided by you, pain medication, once in a while," he talked down to me, instantly I didn't like him.

He opened a large wooden door at the end of the balcony, a woman on a bed in the centre of the room reclined back, I could see the top of her thigh with her dress pulled up, I averted my eyes, not wanting to cause her any embarrassment, but she didn't seem embarrassed, she turned on the bed, her confidence was staggering. She slowly stood in her ruffled black dress. I could smell tobacco in the room, and an unearthly smell of spirits.

"She sent a child?" her husky voice was derisive. Already I could tell I wouldn't like it here. "Bloody hell, John, what am I to do with her?"

She turned away from me. I couldn't let this opportunity go. "Ma'am, please, I can work, I can do whatever you need me to do, please."

She looked at me over her shoulder, her dark eyes stretched into my soul. "What is your vice?"

I shook my head; I didn't understand what she was asking. She rushed towards me, grabbing my purse. She was a cruel woman. Taking my bottle, I reached for it, but she swung around.

"John, hold her," she called. John jumped forward, holding me back from clawing her eyes out at the sight of her holding my bottle.

She drifted towards me, the black lace shawl around her shoulders dropped. After she'd read the bottle, she came close to me. "Where did you get this?"

"From the chemist, for my pain."

"Oh, dear," she pouted her lips, mocking me. "We all have pain here. I can get you something better than this, something you couldn't give to an infant." She straightened up, passing the bottle back to me. "If you wish to work here, then we have a few conditions, this will become your home, we clothe you, feed you, bathe you, everything, you only leave if I say you can leave, if you leave without me saying I will never allow you back and you will pay back your wage for the years spent here." She was abrupt, she didn't frighten me, she terrified me. "Now, we will provide you with our medication for your pain." She had no feelings towards me, nothing for the sake of my soul. "We will send your wage to your guardians or parents."

"I don't have any. I only have Gladys and Thomas, the fishmongers on Fisher Gate."

"Very well, then we can either place it into trust or have it sent to them. Which would you prefer?"

"I would rather it go to them; this was only to hold us through the winter..."

She burst with a deep laugh, "Oh, child, you do amuse me, believe me, by the time the winter is through, you will beg to stay." I highly doubted it. "Now, I hear from your guardian you could help here by ways of entertainment?"

I shuddered, "Well, I do sing, I sang in the choir in Sutton."

"Oh," she seemed disappointed. I could hear John sniggering behind me. "Well, Gladys said you have a talent, so come on, let's hear it."

I could not get my bearings. "I don't know what to sing... I would usually have a sheet or something."

"She said you sing shanties, but I suppose this is a place for gentlemen not drunken louts, so, what do you think they should hear?"

She was testing me, forcing me to dig deep and show her what I believe a gentleman was, I thought as hard as I could of the perfect song, this was a place for gentlemen, but it was also a place for business, a place where a man, wished to be entertained and feel relaxed at the same time. I tried my luck. I had thought all I could. A full rendition of Rule Britannia could sway them, Thomas Arne had some wonderful works, and I knew them all.

"When Britain first, at heaven's command, Arose from out the azure main, Arose from out the azure main,
This was the charter, the charter of the land.
And Guardian Angels sang this strain,
Rule Britannia, Britannia rules the waves, Britons never, never, never will be slaves..."
Holding her hands up from my deafening soprano voice, she stood back.

"Good lord woman!" commented John, "We try to keep order within the chambers, honestly I think you will do well. However, we will choose the songs from now on."

"I agree," she huffed as she turned back toward the window.

John escorted me to the back door. I had only a week to consider my options. I would speak with Tom and Gladys on my return. I did not like that place, I felt strange, a belonging there seemed to catch me the moment I stepped in, but a danger followed me in there, 'twas not a friendly place, but I would not be there to make friends, I would be there to entertain, to rouse the gentlemen of the chambers, to fill their heads and hearts with song, I belonged upon that stage.

I made my way towards the Weekday, a small lady passing smiled at me, I recognised her face from the Weekday, but I said nothing, I still felt shaken from the Lion's Chambers, that place was a place of Gentlemen, and as God as my witness I would bag my own before I reached eighteen.

CHAPTER FIVE DEN OF INIQUITY

She was insistent. Gladys; I told her everything about what I'd seen, what that woman had done, and John, but still she seemed to think I would have a great standing in the town if I were to work there. I wasn't so sure; I felt cold when I thought about that place. A sickness had fallen over me. I was reaching for my bottle more than usual. My nerves would hit me each time I thought of that stage. What they wanted to use me for was something I had dreamt of, but now it had arrived. I was fearful of myself, my talent. I knew I could sing; I had been told enough times in Sutton that my voice was to rouse the angels, but I still doubted I could sing in a town such as Nottingham, where such ills had happened to me, my need to find a gentleman blinded me, failing to see the struggle upon the streets of Nottingham.

I heard a legend once, a tale of a man called Robin Hood, who would feed the poor from the pockets of the rich, his sheltered life in Sherwood forest kept him guarded from the sheriffs men, since arriving here I had seen his failure, 'twas a wonderful story to sit by a fire and listen to upon an evening, but when seeing the streets of Nottingham myself I realised these people needed a false hope just to keep them going. Perhaps the Lions Chambers were exactly that. They were my false hope to find favour among the people here, and finally find me a gent who would take me as his own.

Gladys helped by packing my bag. I had brought hardly anything with me from Sutton, but I had collected a few bits while being in the town.

"Now, don't forget, you can leave any time, so long as you get the approval of your employer," said Gladys, she stood upon the step of the house, seeing me away that morning, I still felt ill, I had been alone from the moment my parents died, but I never truly felt it, now however, 'twas the loneliest feeling I had ever felt, a feeling of fear, excitement, rage, and need seemed to fill me, my bottle was almost empty from the amount I had taken that morning.

"Worry not, Rose, we can come by the Lion and see you if you wish," Tom stood behind

Gladys, 'twas like a moment from a book, as they see their child away for schooling in the larger towns and cities, but I was no child and this was no school, the Lion's Chambers Gentleman's Club would become my new home for the winter, and if that woman had her way I would stay there for life.

The street was dull, the calling from the bells of St Peters church seemed to chill me that morning, a soft humming of conversation drifted across the road from some men making their way down Carter Gate, the crunching of gravel beneath cart wheels echoed through the daunting streets. My breath steadied as I walked.

"Rose!" I heard someone call out, "Rose, please wait!"

I twisted to see Cynthia rushing towards me. Stopping in the street, I stood to the side to wait for her.

"What has you out?"

"Fate." Her reply was odd. I didn't believe in such nonsense. "Rose, I need to warn you of something," the worry of her tone unnerved me, "they will not be kind to you there, they will not treat you right, please, Rose, I can help you find work, just stay away from the Lion."

"I can't. They offered me work. I shall have my own room, my own clothes they will buy for me, and it will keep Gladys and Tom through the winter."

"No, they can keep themselves," her tone deepened, her worry heightened, "Rose, please, just come with me. Gladys and Tom are not the people you think they are."

I felt the hairs on my arms stand on end. "And who are you to say such things?" she offended every part of me, "you weren't there, you weren't there when Gladys helped me, you weren't there when Tom taught me all I needed to know of his trade, you were nowhere, sat on your filthy throne in your abode, awaiting your next client, why should I heed the warning of a whore?" I felt my brow wrinkle to a look of disgust.

Her teeth gritted, "You're right, Rose, I am nothing but a whore, but an honest one, one without fear of reprisal, one who has been like you, wanting nothing more than to be an honest wife to an honest man, but I did not sully those who tried to help me, I simply declined, politely, like any lady should."

Her scalding of me was fair. I was cruel to a woman who had shown nothing but concern, but I allowed my anger to guide me. My mind was not my own.

"I appreciate your concern, but kindly leave me. I have a duty to those who protected me, and a duty to those who offered me a chance."

Turning to leave, I could feel her still stood there. I knew she watched my every step as I left towards Hockley. Every bone in my body told me to run, even my mind argued with me, why would Cynthia warn me of such things, her accusations towards Gladys and Tom hurt me so, but what reason did she have to hurt me, it seemed so strange, so odd, that a common whore would attempt to save the innocence of a child she knew nothing about.

The early morning walk seemed dull. Upon reaching Goose Gate, a new hope seemed to renew. A fresh autumn sun warmed me as I stood by the staff door. I waited for a while before I knocked, taking in all the delights of the surrounding streets, filled with muck and filth, men calling across the street, I would not miss this place, my home for the winter would be within the chambers, whether Cynthia approved.

John met me at the door. "Morning, John," I greeted as politely as I could. He did not look pleased.

"You shall refer to me as Mr. Bentley," his twisted lip showed I disgusted him. "Do you not have anything else to wear?"

His derisive look made me feel as small as a beggar. "I came here with little; I chose my best dress for this occasion." I tried to hold a smile to Mr. Bentley, but I could feel it wavering.

I did not like him; I did not like that woman, and I did not like this place, but I had no choice.

"We will find something more befitting your purpose," his smile was cold, taunting. Opening the door for me, I made my way in, taking one last breath of the air outside and my last moment of freedom.

Had I known then what I did now, I would never have worn that dress. Mr. Bentley hurried through the bar area of the gentleman's club, a strong smell of pipe smoke stuck with me, but all I could feel in the air was a bitterness, sickness gripped my stomach with each heavy step I took up the stairs, everything I did seemed to be followed by the eyes of the servers in the main bar, well-dressed men glided through, patrons had not arrived in the chambers yet, they would be busy with business that day, giving them ample time to clean the chambers before their masters returned.

The ill feeling did not ease within my gut as we came to the top of the stairs, the thick red carpet appeared clean that day from the thousand footsteps, the dark wood banister had a fresh coat of wax for their masters to place their hands upon. Everything in that place spoke of the lavish extravagance a gentleman wished to enjoy. It turned my heart away from the want I used to feel for a gentleman husband.

Upon arriving at the top of the balcony, a darkness filled the open corridor. We whisked our way to a door at the very end. The thick wooden door made of a dark wood. I had a feeling the extravagance would reach beyond the hall and into every room. Showing me in, Mr. Bentley opened the door with one arm stretched. I stepped in front of him, looking at the room inside. The woman caught my eye, reclined on the bed, a bare thigh showed through her black lace dress. Her figure was slim, tall, and daunting, her red hair cascaded past her waist. She did not seem to care for the etiquette of proper ladies.

She slowly stood to greet me in the room. The autumn sun poured through the window behind her, heavy red curtains swept along the bottom of the floor.

"So, you saw sense." her comment unhinged me, as much as the husk within her throat. "Come, sit with me," she gave a low nod of her head to Mr. Bentley, who still stood with the door. My heart quickened. I clutched my small bag to the front of me, holding on to the only comfort I knew.

The room was a large open expanse, containing a large bed, to the left a large washroom with a dresser to the side beside the door, and close to the window was a small table with two large, rather ornate chairs, a comfortable leather covered them. As she sat upon the bed, my body crumpled, watching her sit with such grace. "I would rather stand, ma'am."

"Oh, Rose, call me Claudia, although I am your madam. My girls are as friends to me." She rose from the bed, creeping towards me, her body swelled. Reaching out, she took a curl of my hair. "We have blond, red." She flicked her proud locks of hair to the back of her. "But this is something we haven't seen for a while here; the gentlemen of the chambers favour the exotic."

"Exotic?" It shocked me. Claudia circled me, taking in every inch of my body. Her eyes violated me. "You think me exotic?"

"Well, the ladies of Ireland would bring with them curled locks of fawn hair, but yours is a rare type, the curls you hold, the deep thickness of the hair, and your deep dark eyes," she raised her head as she arrived back in front of me, looking down to me with her eyes. "Tell me of your parents, child."

"They both died, a long time ago."

My shattering reply sent her back to the bed. She lost her grace as she sat. Tapping the bed, I ambled towards her, reluctant at first, I placed my bag on the ground and sat upon the red sheets beside her. The large wooden bed was a comfort to me. It was much larger, much grander than I expected. They usually saved the intricate patterns of the headboard for the more extravagant houses and manors.

"We all lose things in this life, Rose. One thing we are all guaranteed, is death. Stop reaching for life, when it only leads to the end."

"That is a very grim thought."

"No, 'tis an honest thought, I had parents too, they died when I was young, like you, they sent me from there to the workhouse, where I grew into a lady, convinced I would see the world with a good husband, a gentleman, that is what they teach you," her voice was soft, alluring, what I did not expect was to see my likeness within her. "When I left the workhouse, they promised me duty, until they abandoned me..." her eyes stiffened to the front of her, a swirling temptress unravelled in front of me. "I was a lady once too until I became the whore I am today."

Her eyes softened as she looked at me. "That is not what you are, surely. This is a gentleman's chambers, a place of good men..."

"You see gentlemen, where I see animals, Rose, I shall always be honest, I will not place you to work with those Gentlemen who have too many hands, your work will be as companion, here," she reached to the side of the bed, taking a small bottle, it was a pretty bottle, swirling patterns along the outside mesmerised me. "That will be your new companion. You shall be The Rose of Nottingham, here to entertain men to your fullest ability. My duty is different. I would never turn you into me."

I took a moment to think, wondering what I would actually be doing. "Tell me, what do you expect of me?"

"To sing of an evening, to allow our gents here to relax, following that you shall retire to your chambers and entertain those who wish to have your company. Anything beyond that is my duty."

My heartbeat was fast as she handed me the bottle, taking the lid from the bottle, she softly cupped her hand under my chin, opening my mouth, a single drop hit my tongue, I had never felt it before, such peace hit me, a euphoria like none other, soft grasses licked my delicate skin, a warm summer sun graced the grass below me. Trees swayed in the breeze. With every breath I took, I felt it, a deep pleasure I had never felt. I wanted more, and Claudia was there to give it to me.

The first night there I they left me alone, I opened the door to my room, peering to those below me, many of the gentlemen were older men, some were young, men of the law, the sheriffs' men seemed to fill the chambers that evening, a soft moon lit the streets below, thick bars on the outside of the window only allowed for a small opening.

"Are you ready?" Mr. Bentley stood outside of my door.

"I believe so," I replied with a wobbling voice. I could hardly sing with such nerves.

"Good gracious, girl, take some of the vice Claudia gave you. I expect to see you upon the stage in less than 5 minutes."

"And what am I to sing?"

He opened the door further. I wore the only dress I could find which had they left in the wardrobe to the back of my chambers. A green satin and lace bodice, beneath was a long green and lace flowing skirt. I believed I looked divine, and given the look on John's face, he did too.

"We have decided something you may know well, we have a small ensemble, just a few songs, there is a sheet upon the stage, Rule Britannia followed by Heart of Oak, we have an admiral joining us this evening, so it is only fitting we mark the occasion."

He slammed the door, and I could hardly breathe, I was being thrown to the lions, if I did not please them now, I never would, my voice was good but were it good enough to entertain those who had seen the greatest shows within London theatres, I would never be as good as those women or men who trained tirelessly for years perfecting every note they sang, I was nothing compared to them.

The blood red curtains poured open, the stage lights hit me, I could feel my body become weaker, a sweat misted upon my brow, I looked to the faces glaring towards me, the flickering flames of the stage lights were taunting, eyes from every angle were all on me. A small ensemble to the side gave the first note from a violin.

It was now or never. I could not sing, I could not feel my voice, my throat was dry, and so I did the only thing I believed would work. Holding up my hand, I held my head high.

"Sir, would you be so kind to fetch me some water?" I asked the server who stood beside the stage facing the audience. He turned toward me. I raised my brows at him, forcing him from the stage. "Apologies, Gentlemen." I looked around the room at the smiling faces. "I believe you are here to be entertained. A cackling cat is hardly entertainment," I mocked, receiving a muffle of laughter from the crowd.

The moments passed with the talking pleasantly to the audience. John stood by the bar, whispering into the ears of patrons, waiting for me to preform my magic.

"As you may all be aware," I spoke again, harbouring their attention further, "while this is new to these wonderful chambers, I have gained some experience, and so, I wish to add to this evening's sheet, your manager clearly does not know good talent when he sees it." I was a pleaser. Given the winks and laughter from the crowd, I had them in the palm of my hands. I did not know who this woman on stage was, but I belonged there.

Walking towards my ensemble, I whispered to the front, "Are you familiar with Handel?" they nodded nervously. "Then we shall begin, Gentlemen, with Lascia ch'io pianga from Rinaldo."

I felt their collective concern, as I began my aria, the room fell silent, not a single whisper, not a single man stood to move, the servers froze, even the curtains beside the stage did not move, I had silenced them, and I tried so hard, I could have been anyone upon that stage, but now I felt it, I was myself; I was exactly where I belonged. Adoring applause hit after my first aria, I lightened with John's insistence of Rule Britannia, followed by another chat with my audience.

"I believe we have an esteemed guest with us this evening, not to say you are not all esteemed guests," I chalked. "Admiral Barton-Hove?" I nervously questioned. I saw John at the bar fling himself forward. He panicked, whereas the tall and rather dashing Admiral stood proudly from his seat. "Admiral," I held my hand out to him. "If you would wish to join me for a Hearty Oak?"

"Of course, Ma'am," he seemed uncomfortable, he leant towards me, "I

apologise, but I do not know your name?" his
tightened lips amused me.

"I am Rose, Admiral, Rose of
Nottingham." I began our shanty, something he
would've heard sang a thousand times aboard
his ship, but always too professional to join in.
The chambers were a place of safety to those of
higher ranks. By the end of my performance, I
could tell they loved me.

I was enjoying my stay there; my time so
far had taken me on a journey which had
rendered my tincture useless. The evening
outside quietened. I heard the handle to my door
turn, looking to the shadow which entered.
Claudia always looked like a woman of
perfection, although she did not tie or curl her
hair, 'twas something the gentlemen clearly liked.

"Your evening so far?" she asked,
casually making her way in.

"It has been pleasant, thank you."

"Well, Mr. Bentley had plans to teach
you better, but you seem to know, you surprise
me, Rose, you captivated them all. It often takes a
while before our girls can speak properly to our
patrons."

"The sisters taught me well..."

"Gods whores..." she abruptly turned,
frightening me. "They dedicate their lives to a
lie." Her words send shivers through me, unable
to look at her. "If you believe in god child, then

that is something you are quite welcome to hold on to, but believe me, god has no place within these walls, the nuns of the workhouse know how to speak to men who pretend to be something they're not, behind closed doors we're all different, 'tis your duty to loosen tongues, allow them to speak freely to you, knowing their secrets, their frustrations remain only with you, you will be a whore of words," her laughing unnerved me.

"I have no belief in god."

Slumping onto the bed beside me, she looked to my head upon my pillow, resting her head on her wrist, tracing her finger around my face.

"Men are monsters, Rose, the man who had you as his own. Was he a gentleman?"

I whiffled my head, not knowing how she knew. I did not ask. My voice broke with a whisper, "No."

"He was to someone." My eyes drifted towards her; a curled upper lip spelt hatred. "Some are good, kind men, some are harsh undertakers of chastity, but gentleman, Rose, they no longer exist. The quicker you realise this, the easier your search will become."

Standing from the bed, she lifted my bag from the floor. "What are you doing?"

Unclasping my bag, she took my nightgown out. "I told you before you arrived, we feed you, bathe you, clothe you, you have no need for this now, as for the dress you wore here, burn it, or remain a child of the workhouse, forever clinging to a hope that does not exist." She abruptly turned and left the room. Turning in my bed I could've burst with tears, hearing a click I shot from the bed, realising she had locked me in, frantically I pulled at the handle, twisting, and turning as hard as I could, tears blinded my eyes, I was their prisoner now, but I would keep my dress, my reminder of who I was, and what I came here to do.

The morning brought an icy breeze from the crack in the window. Opening my misted eyes, I slowly bought myself to sit on the edge of the bed. My eyes were heavy and head full of a deep regret.

The lock on my door rattled. I remained still on the bed. "I apologise, I always lock the doors." Claudia stepped in. I did not turn my head to greet her. I felt angry with her. "Oh, come on child, you will thank me later."

Twisting my eyes toward her, I felt a cold shiver run through me. "I highly doubt it."

"You are not our prisoner, Rose. You came here of your own free will, to better the lives of your guardians, who would starve without your wage, as many do in winter." A deep truth in her voice shook me. The thought of Gladys and Tom suffering hurt me deeply. I had a duty to fulfil, my duty was to them. "So, would you like to see your new gowns?"

I slowly turned my head, nodding slightly. Claudia looked to the door. A short woman, wearing a black maid's uniform, bought a long clothes rail. The dresses were not what I expected. Red, pink, the deepest colour turquoise I ever saw was all upon the rail. Unexpected colours of such delight hit me. My eyes were awash with colour. But the dresses were new from the ones I knew. They were strange styles, not the garments they would see me on the streets wearing. The bodices were tight, whale bone woven into the fabric made it utterly beautiful. Lush silk skirts were long to the back and short to the front.

I stood in front of the long mirror in the room's corner. An extensive wardrobe with a lock would hold my new garments. I looked at my body. I never realised I would be desirable before, but the deep blue bodice showed a womanly figure. The skirt made me look tall, slim; I was a woman now, but it was the first time meeting myself.

"Am I to go barefoot?" I mocked, looking at Claudia.

She came toward me, standing behind me she looked at my reflection in the mirror. "You do not need such earthly possessions, Rose." She took a lock of my hair, placing it to the back of me, and allowing me to see a potential I had not seen in myself before. "You are to remain here, in the realm of power." Taking my shoulders, she turned me to face her. "Do you know what power you hold, Rose?"

I was bashful. "Very little, if any."

Her red lips tightened, "You have more power than any man who steps into these chambers, you are a woman, Rose, men are frightened of that, that is why they use their strength, they fear the power we hold over their souls and hearts." Drifting around me, she took my hand, guiding me towards the bed. "Soon you will see the power you hold over them, and when you do you will never wish to leave this place, you will never wish to receive shoes, not when you live in the den of iniquity, you reside among the angels."

"Claudia, you speak of power, of iniquity, I sang for them, that was all, nothing more." She held a finger to my lips, trapping my insecurities.

"I will hear no more doubt from you, Rose, you are a woman of power, and you will show them that, only then will you fill your role here, to speak, to listen, to enjoy the company of gentlemen, even the boring ones must be as entertaining as a summers fete, your duty is to act, Rose, make them love you, make every one of them fall madly in love with you, then show them your power when you show them the door."

I doubted I would ever be ready for such an undertaking. Her confidence filled the room. Claudia would become my guide and mentor, 'twas a den of iniquity, but, 'twas my home, I now resided among angels.

CHAPTER SIX MANIMALS

The chambers were quiet; they spoke of others there, but I was yet to see them, the rooms I passed on my daily commute along the balcony were empty, the nights were silent when the doors closed, but the evenings were busy, the air would light with the sound of my voice. I was their addiction; I only fulfilled their needs. Their ladies left at home so they could enjoy my entertainment within the Lions Chambers. I was still just a girl, but I was different, I was their girl, their good girl, who shared her tincture with them, to me 'twas an addiction, to them, 'twas nothing more than a way to relax into my company, a way to escape the dismal world of business. I heard industry from my window constantly, and it was my gentlemen who were building the town where I now resided.

I did not leave my room often, I had no reason to, meals brought to me upon silver platter, I dined at the small table at my window, always with a white table linen covering, a small bit of lace, my plate was of fine bone china from the Royal Crown Derby, I had expensive taste now, and I had only seen a single winter within the chambers.

My routine was strict. Each morning, I would make my way to the room at the back, nestled by the side of the wardrobe. My washroom was just for me, no sharing, like within the workhouse. Ambling through my quarters, I opened my wardrobe. I had a choice now. The battered pink dress I used to see as beautiful remained in a crumpled pile on the back. Each day, I would receive gifts from my gentlemen. From gingham dresses to the thick, lush fabrics of Scottish tweed, even silk shawls and leather boots and slippers. My life had changed, and my gentlemen had changed it.

The evening brought a mumbled conversation from the bar below as they arrived. My door remained closed until my curtain call. Mr. Bentley failed to bring my usual list of clienteles to me before the festivities began. A light knock on the door had me prepared. They all came for my voice, but they stayed for Rose.

"Evening," I peered around the door to see my old judge Francis, he was always pleasant company, his wife had been suffering of late, and he preferred to leave her to the silence of the house, rather than make demands of her time.

"Good evening, Rose." He stepped in, removing his cloak and jacket. "I see you've chosen my colours this evening."

"I expected to see you, and I know the judge likes his blood red." I had learnt a lot, to flirt, to seduce with words. I was an expert at it now. He made his way into my parlour, a large chair held him comfortably, he liked to sit near the window, watching the detritus outside, 'twas the duty of law men to keep villains off our streets, 'twas the duty of the judge to ensure they never returned.

With the town of Nottingham safely outside my window, 'twas the duty I requested of all my gentlemen to tell me of the town outside. The gossip of the streets drifted to my room daily. Today was the turn of my favourite client.

"I know you have little time before your evening begins. A brief chat will keep me up this evening. The winter ended with little struggle." Francis looked from the window; a melancholy look greyed his face. "You promised to leave the chambers following the winter," he raised his brows with a question, "So, my Rose of Nottingham, will you stay, I wonder?"

Drifting towards him, my red lace trailed on the floor behind me. He preferred a gentle touch for a lady to act as such, but that was outside of my quarters. Here, he liked me to display honesty with my innocence.

"I have wondered this myself," my lungs emptied at the thought of leaving the chambers. "I will make my decision before the month is out."

"It's a harsh truth you must face, Rose. Come, sit with me." I sat beside him, taking my bottle he so desperately looked towards. I took my drop. He did not partake in such things. The judge of the sordid town insisted his head was to remain clear.

"The only truth I face now, is that I was the apprentice of a fishmonger. Now I have a choice, to return to chopping fish, or remain within the chambers, upon the stage."

"If only it were that simple," his quiet voice shook me. "Have you thought if they would even have you back, the workhouses are constantly pouring disadvantaged youth into our streets, they probably have another apprentice by now."

"Well, they wouldn't need one. My wage here keeps them well."

"It keeps them very well, from what I hear."

I sat back, placing my hands on my lap, "And what is it you hear?"

Shaking his head, he was reluctant to speak, but I was his Rose. He would tell me all I needed to know. "You please them with your work here, so pleased. In fact, it is doubtful they would let you return, you know very little of them." He took a breath, breaking his trail of conversation. "I like you, Rose. I do not wish to see you upset. The chambers will always be here to hold you, protect you, and keep you. Should you wish to stay?"

"It is something I shall discuss with Claudia when the chance arises, but for today I wish to hear of you, your troubles of the day."

"My troubles lifted, I'm here now, with my Rose." His wide smile warmed me. He had never been mean to me. He was a kind soul, swept up by the political swill of Nottingham town.

The underhanded ways of law men ruled the town, but something much darker lingered in the halls of the Lions Chambers, something I never wanted to see, or become a part of.

My evening of entertaining saw them in the company of my favourite aria, part of the Zaide opera by the great Mozart. My gentlemen had a feel for me now. They expected conversation upon the stage and in my quarters. They knew my taste matched theirs. Each night, I would see John huddled by the bar, watching in jealousy as I wooed my audience. I do not know why he hated me so, but I felt it from his eyes every night I sang. The crowd would cheer, and he would avoid.

The evening brought a pleasant light, an orange hue cast along the skies of the town, it brought peace, a tranquil abyss in the swirling clouds was a pleasing sight to me, but I could scarcely see anything, my mind was awash with question, the guardians I saw as parents had not been to visit me once, their tongues remained silent, I had known them for a few months before choosing them as my guardians, 'twas a regret I was feeling.

My blood ran warm that evening as Claudia stepped in. She had seen her last gentleman around the hour of midnight. The bells of the churches surrounding chimed a dull and eerie song as my door opened. She always looked perfect; I was noticing more now. At seventeen I saw the womanly form in a much more pleasing eye, my days within the workhouse would see me constantly preying, church on Sundays used to be a time of enjoyment, but now nothing seemed more boring than being sat in a cold stinking church, being preached to of innocence. I lost mine, ruined by one of God's men. God had forsaken me, and now I was forsaking him.

Her beauty was a cause of constant jealousy for me, I loved her long hair, so soft and perfect, her red pouting lips, her shaded pink skin, even the way she sat was something I tried to copy, Claudia had become my guide, my guardian, and I knew she would let nothing bad happen to me.

"You told Francis you would decide within the month?" even her deep voice soothed me.

"I did."

"And have you decided yet?" she looked worried, fiddling with a loose thread of her black lace skirt.

"I have not," pacing the room I tried to think. "They were good to me. I owe them a lot."

"You paid your debt in full, Rose," she slowly stood, taking my hands in her soft, warm palms. "They have another apprentice, Rose. From now on, you still have a choice. Your wage can go to them still, or we can return it to you." I cannot deny it disappointed me; I did not expect Gladys and Tom to move on so fast. "Rose, every year we have a winter. They have seen many before this and always survived..."

"They needed me!" my shouting startled her, but she composed herself, holding my hands tighter.

"When you came here, I promised you I would remain honest, it is a promise I intend to keep, Rose, no matter how harsh it may seem, they do not need you, they are mongers, they bring the girls, and in the winter, they get rid, the chambers only accept the talented ones, you were one of the lucky ones, in the summer they bring more, and so on, and so forth." My heart was pounding in my chest, hoping desperately for a lie. "Rose, you came here just as I did, fifteen years ago. I first saw the inside of these chambers, and one day, you shall look back as I do, and be grateful for what the lions have given you."

My eyes flickered at the thought. The magnitude of their actions disturbed me. "And what of those who you do not accept?"

"You met one, once, her name was Cynthia, her talents were lacking, so taking up her career on Fisher Gate, she now lives on Greyhound Street, until next year when she will again move on, who knows, she could be in Derby or Lincoln, it all depends on what they want."

"Who?"

"This town is darker than you think. Everything comes from the Lions Chambers. Rose, especially our fate. Call it that if you wish, a house of fate, where they decide the futures of many, where your sentences will be read."

"And what is my fate, because it sounds like I have no choice?"

"You have a choice, either remain here or become like Cynthia, a whore of a town, you get to keep the money you make, but it is of greater risk to yourself, the beds of the chambers they gild in gold, so are the whores."

"I am not a whore..."

She squeezed my wrists; I could feel her grip tighten. "You are whatever they say you are, Rose, you do not let them into you as I do, yet, but you give them more than what I give, I've heard you, talking of your time in the workhouse, telling them about your past, telling them of Gladys and Tom, the pathetic life you had before here, which is now gone, tell me, Rose, what will you tell them when your stories of innocence run out? Uum, will you tell of your addiction, your vile need for the liquid you carry, I may be a standard whore. I give them my body, you give them your soul."

Dropping my wrists, she left towards the bed. "I do my duty in this place. I provide companionship..."

"Companionship," she spat, "'tis nothing but a poor excuse. You are not doing your duty, you enjoy it. The stage is yours and yours alone. You are the talk of the town, Rose." I did not know about this. I remained in the chambers, sheltered from the outside world.

"I didn't know, I only know what they tell me..."

"You tell them of your innocence, Rose. Have you told your gentlemen your full past?" She saw me shudder. Placing her hand on her chin, she turned. "Oh wait, have you told them that? That a man, a gentleman nonetheless, took your innocence from you, like a thief in the night he took everything from the innocent Rose, you didn't tell them did you, that you are no longer pure..." she came close to me, I felt her breath upon my neck, I hated myself, the chambers had ended my hate for who I was, but now, she had awoken it. "You didn't take that, Rose, he did, and that is why your duty changes," her voice changed, her cruel tone softened. "From now on, you listen to them, everything they tell you, everything they say, your story has ended, Rose, you're here now, and here you will stay."

"With my service in the chambers remaining, could you could grant me leave?"

"Certainly not," she tightened her lips, "Rose, one day you will walk these streets freely, for now you need to realise the truth, they used you, and we gained you, Gladys and Tom are dead to you now, do not return there, or your final breath will be upon a rope."

A death threat was not something I was expecting. The chambers darkened that night and from that day; the light did not return.

Queen of the Night was never a favourite of mine, but I was raging. Mozart would make Claudia clear of how I felt that night, screaming

the aria from the stage the audience was silently
shocked, awe-stricken, and certainly impressed.

There was more to the chambers than I first
thought, with every passing hour I realised this
was more than a place for gentlemen to relax
after a hard day of business, 'twas a place to
gamble, but money was not their prize, they
gambled with the lives of people, those who were
not as wealthy as they were, those who struggled
to make a living, they saw them as useless, and
worthy of a place in the marshes.

Keeping their hands clean in the business
of building the town was of great importance to
them, they handed the dirty work to the lawmen,
the sheriff's men, and my Francis, he had been
absent of late, over a month had passed without
his presence, it was a hard time within the
chambers for me.

They would come in their droves, talk
business within the halls. They filled the bar with
talk of detritus and scum. How better to
extinguish the needy, than at the hands of the law.
The poorest of the poor, driven to crime. The
sheriff's men were excellent in their duty. I would
hang from the balcony, listening to those below,
speaking of what better ways to lure the needy.
They called it baiting, placing half decent food in
the reach of a starving man, only to catch him
desperately reaching for it. From there he would

see the Gaol, Francis would deliver his sentence, and death upon Gallows hill would follow. They were not gentlemen. To call them animals would be an insult to a diseased sow. They were manimals, monsters who claimed to be something they were not.

"Why do you allow it?" Francis sat upon my parlour chair. He had been quiet, 'twas his first visit there in a month. He did not wish to hear of my concerns.

"The town is full to bursting with men like the ones who hurt you, Rose. I am simply here to protect all ladies, not only you, but my duty also runs much deeper than you realise."

I sensed an anger. His voice shook as he spoke. A harshness to his words was something I was not used to. Kneeling to the front of him, I placed my hands on his lap, trying desperately to comfort him.

"Where have you been?"

He lowered his eyes; I could feel his grief. "My wife, she has suffered illness most of her life, she is no longer in pain, she remains in the arms of angels."

"You loved her, didn't you?"

His eyes raised toward me, "Once, I did yes, but years are harsh, they often take more than they give."

"Did you have children with her?" I stood, taking a seat beside him.

"I would have, if god had allowed," he gave a fatherly look to me, and then I knew, he hated him, just as much as me, I had my innocence taken, and Francis had his future taken. "We had two girls and three boys, one of my girls died in infancy, the boys, two were born sleeping and the third, he died of a fever..."

"And the other girl?"

He shook his head, unable to speak of it. "She was a different story, one I do not wish to speak of. She is no longer now."

"I'm so sorry, Francis, the world is cruel, filled with unfairness."

"But one thing has benefited me, you're still here. Even in my absence you remain."

"They told me the truth, what the chambers really are, and what I would become if I chose to leave." His eyes drifted about the room, not knowing how to respond. "I am safe here, Francis, my gentlemen keep me safe."

"Yes, yes, we do, and we always will. Now, I have an early start on the morrow, I shall see you in the evening, I hope. Tomorrow is her funeral. She shall reside at St Mary's, a place where I can always see her."

I saw him to the door. He left a sadness in the room that evening. I could feel his loss hours after he had left.

The oil lamps in the bar dulled. Ambling from the balcony, I saw Mr. Bentley instructing the staff as they closed for the evening.

"Mr. Bentley," I called to him.

"Evening, Rose."

"Mr. Bentley, I need to inform you of some terrible news."

His eyes narrowed; he made his way toward the stairs. "Continue your work," he called to the servers. He came to the top of the stairs. Placing his arm around my waist, he guided me back into my room. "What is it?" he closed the door behind him.

"It's Francis, you may have heard. His wife passed. Her funeral is tomorrow at St Mary's."

"Oh, that is awful, thank you for letting me know, I will be sure to lie on more provisions tomorrow for him."

He turned to leave, but I had to stop him. I had to ask. "There was one more thing." He let the handle go. "I was rather hoping, I could go?"

"Go where?" his scornful face returned.

"To her funeral."

He laughed at me, harder and harder. The more he laughed, the more it hurt. "Francis sees you as his mistress. To have your mistress at the funeral of your wife is wildly inappropriate." His sniggering continued, but I did not laugh.

"Rose, you are nothing to him. You provide an escape from court. Your place by the side of Francis Monrow is firmly within these walls, no further."

"Mr. Bentley," I harshly replied, angered by his laughter, "one of our members has lost a loved one, and you laugh at this, you laugh in the face of his dead wife, I was never a mistress to Francis, he is one of the few gentlemen here." I had not noticed his hand had released the latch of the door; it slowly opened. "He is the magistrate of this town, and you accuse him of such behaviour. I am sickened by your conduct, your laughter at a man in heartbreak and pain, one of our most trusted members..."

"What is the meaning of this?" burst Claudia, hurrying into the room, and closing the door behind her.

"John believes it amusing that Francis has lost his wife to illness, her funeral is tomorrow..."

"Is this true?" her look of disgust towards John pleased me.

"It is not true. I was laughing at the thought of her going. His mistress arriving at the funeral of his wife would make him a laughingstock of this town."

"She is not his mistress, Francis has never dabbled in such iniquities." Her argument was valid, but what she did next, I did not expect. "Excuse yourself, Mr. Bentley, I will not have this kind of behaviour within my home, this is my business, and the Lion's Chambers do not welcome such ill-informed people."

"Madam Claudia, I apologise, but sending her to the funeral of his dead wife would be inappropriate..."

"For him maybe, for the chambers, certainly not, you work for me, now leave, and watch your tongue, should a word of the chambers leave your mouth, you know your fate."

"Madam, please, I need this work..."

"You should think of that before making accusations towards a judge. Now go before I have you removed," her deep rumbling voice shook me to the core. Her anger with him was clear.

I watched his hands tremble as he left. "Claudia, I did not expect that response..."

She abruptly turned, "It would be a poor idea to be at the side of Francis during the funeral of his wife, however, being at the church will show the Lions Chambers shows support and gratitude to our patrons, go, tomorrow, I grant you leave."

I felt my body melt and stiffen all at once. An emptiness hit me, knowing I could leave and never return.

My feelings were twisted and ill, my past paled compared to how I felt now, I had heard

Claudia correctly, she was the one, the chambers were hers, but she was not what I believed she was, a prisoner just like me, the chambers left her deluded, she believed she had some control over the manimals who ran her, the board members controlled her every move, they would not be happy with her firing John Bentley, the backlash would be something we would all feel.

CHAPTER SEVEN THE FORGOTTEN

A light summer drizzle misted the windows to the chambers. My window remained as wet as my face, but I did not cry for losing someone I did not know. I cried for my freedom. My wages would be mine now, Gladys and Tom would continue to sell girls they gained from the workhouse, but now my wages were my own, I had very little in my purse, 'twould be enough to see me to the Weekday, to a small bakery I had missed since being in the chambers.

Claudia waited by the back door, ready to escort me out with a warning to carry in my heart.

"Good morning," she greeted as I came to the door, wearing a smart tweed dress cut toward the floor. "You look well this morning."

"I feel well, Claudia, thank you." She walked with me toward the street.

"I did not intend for you to see any of that, but at least the chambers will be right by this evening. Return in time for your show. The stage always awaits you, Rose."

She did not warn me, simply reminded me, my thoughts of running were simply idiotic, I had something every woman in my position wanted, I had all eyes on me, every night, I would silence a hundred voices with my single voice, they adored me, so much so they would pay simply to spend a half hour in my company, I was everything to the chambers and more, and the chambers were my home, even stepping to the cold and dismal streets I felt the pull from the empowering building behind me, not wanting me to go, like a child or pet, the Lions Chambers needed me, and I needed them.

My first appointment would see me to St Mary's church, where the burial of Charlotte Monrow would take place at nine in the morn. I expected to see many that day, but few were there. The mourners who arrived were each well dressed. They looked to be awfully familiar with Francis, but each kept their distance. I struggled to understand why.

Stood by the grey stone wall of the church I could not move, I did not wish for those with Francis to see me, I simply needed his eyes to realise my presence, 'twas insisted by Claudia I remain within the shadows, the large gravestones provided plenty of cover, however, I did not notice his eyes glance towards me. I hurried toward the gate before Francis left with his entourage, remaining by the iron gates as he glanced towards me, giving a tight smile. I had done my duty, Claudia would be pleased.

The streets that day remained blighted by misting rain. My freedom was irresistible to me. The slow amble along the rain torn streets brought about pleasure I never thought possible. Arriving towards the Weekday I froze, a scent of fish sullied the air, my mind wandered, I had trusted Gladys and Tom, treated them as I would my family and they had me taken by the chambers. Wandering away from the Weekday I walked through the tight walls of Pepper Street, and on toward Peck Lane, the large market square would hide me from prying eyes, and I would have a choice.

The square was busy, filled with crying children and calling men and women, an overwhelming noise of animals bleated in the afternoon rain. I knew how they felt, locked within their pens, waiting to be sold on to their new masters. I felt sorry for those poor creatures, the large wooden pens held them tight together, a few lambs nestled within one of them, void of mud and muck, the farmer had placed a canvas over the pen to keep them from the rain, he was one of the good farmers who cared for his stock, he looked after their welfare, and that is what the chambers had done for me.

I was a lamb to slaughter once, Gladys
and Tom were the farmers who gave me to a new
master, taking all the profits they could, but the
chambers had shown me that not all masters are
bad, Claudia had been kind to me, she did not
see fit me lying with gentlemen as she did; it
made me wonder why, but she was just like me
once, a lost and lonely girl, one of the forgotten.

As I stood within the busy market, I
turned to see the chaos, where it a year before I
would've been reaching for my bottle, but a new
hope sprung upon me that day, a hope that I had
found my place within Nottingham, 'twas not a
place many desired, but I had my gentlemen
there, I had my quarters, my clothes and my
meals, they gave me everything and asked for
nothing in return, to be the company for some
men was all she had ever asked of me, she even
helped with my addiction, providing stronger
tincture than Gladys ever did, Claudia, and the
chambers had become my unlikely saviour, I
would be a fool to run now, but I should've.

So many greeted me that day.
Gentlemen tilted their hats as I walked through
the street. I struggled to understand why but
would give a nod as they did, 'twas the proper
way of a lady. The chambers did not seem so
dark now. The grey stone I remember so vividly
had changed. The rain had washed a layer of dust
from the light sandstone. I stood in the street for

some time looking at the building which housed me. I still would not use the front door. I remained in my duty, using the back door. I did not realise just how much rain my dress had taken on. I dripped through the bar, up the stairs, and into my warm room.

Upon seeing Claudia, my gratitude towards her grew. She stood by the fire. A member from downstairs had made a hearty log fire, ready for my return.

"You did well," she complimented, seeing me attempt to take the wet cloak from my arms. She helped. "I hope to see Francis this evening. Did he seem well to you?"

"He seemed well, but he was there with friends. I am sure they will look after him."

"Those are no friends," her smirk worried me, hoping he would not be lonely in his age. "Francis has no friends, only acquaintances, the people you would've seen today were most likely his home-staff, he has many, given the care she needed before her passing." Folding my cloak over her arm ready to be dried downstairs, her look of pride turned to a look as warm as love. "You did well."

"Thank you," a thought hit me. Instantly, I turned, "but, how do you know?"

"I had you followed," her snigger unnerved me, "he said he believed you were going to run for a moment, but saw sense."

"Why would you have me followed, Claudia? Do you not trust me?"

"I do trust you," her brows raised towards me, and eyes softened. "Trust is everything, but so is freedom, loyalty, Rose, 'tis all we ask, and 'tis very little, but you proved to me today I can trust you to return home," she slowly came to me, placing her warm hands upon my cold shoulders. "I'm proud of you, Rose, don't be angry either, 'twas not a test, 'twas a simple exercise, ensuring your safety is all. We protect you here, and we all wish to keep it that way."

Before she left, I blurted the words, "I just want to make you proud."

"And you do," she softly replied. The love she showed in her eyes spoke to me. She genuinely loved my being there, and this was my home now.

Returning from my stage, I retired into my room, changing into a more comfortable dress and gown. Smoke from the rooftops filled the skies that evening. 'twas a light evening, even though the rain placed a damp chill in the air. Slowly, my door opened, my first client had arrived, a young man, by the name of Jonathan, he was a lawman, a man I always tried to extract the better side from, I knew his duty, and he was not a gentleman.

"I saw you in the town earlier," his comment seemed bitter. I always wore green for

Jonathan. It seemed to calm him, but this evening, I doubted anything would calm his anger.

"I was, 'twas an enjoyable change, one I needed."

"You dislike the chambers?"

"Of course I do, but staying in these walls gets one frustrated..."

"Hmm," he huffed, taking a seat by the window. He waited for me to remove his shoes. Resting his fist upon his chin, he slumped in the chair. "Frustration, you do not know, child," he murmured.

"Well, it sounds as though you have had a hard day," I tried to calm him, knowing his temper I knew his triggers, able to shoot towards one like an angry bull. I would need to tread carefully that evening. "Let me try to make that better for you, to show you how much we appreciate you in your duty." I reached to my bottle, offering it to him as he held his hand out in refusal. I did not want to seem rude, so placed it onto the table. "I felt safe upon the streets," he glared towards me from the corner of his eye, "the law does a fine job at keeping ladies safe."

He relaxed his hand, placing it to the side of him. "You think you're safe?" he gave a smirk. I knew he had a plan for that evening, otherwise he would not be there. "When I first saw you, the rat child on Fisher Gate, taken by a monster, I knew then, you would end up here, or one of the neighbours."

"What makes you so sure of that?"

"Your mannerisms, I don't deny were it not for his actions and your misfortune in life you would've made a fine lady, Rose, fate was not on your side, but what was on your side was your training, your skill with words, 'twas that evening that Tom came to the back door of the chambers, to talk to Claudia about transferring you." His smile was cruel. It was my first-time hearing this. I knew my being here involved them, but I neglected to realise just what hand they had played in my injuries.

"Jon, you have always been honest with me, and I thank you for that. Will you be honest with me now?" His brows rose, giving a single nod. "Did Gladys and Tom have a part in what happened to me?"

A grin to the side of his mouth worried me. "Perhaps, perhaps not, but they took their opportunity, you needed no kind of pain relief, your injuries, as you said, were not minor, but injuries of the heart and mind are different to those of the body, Rose, they played a part in your addiction."

"My addiction?" I looked at the bottle, lost for words I simply glared at it.

"The streets fill with hate and filth, Rose. I come here to escape that, but even here I'm reminded of it. Everyone within the Lions Chambers has had something happen to them. That was why they formed the chambers. Men of good reputation, who came from money, wealth, and good breeding, all who had seen some misfortune at the hands of others, they built the chambers to discuss their revenge and cure the streets of filth."

"Everyone?" my question rattled him, looking directly into his eyes.

"If you wish to know more, you'd better ask them, but prepare yourself for a world of pain, Rose."

"Then what of you?"

His silence unnerved me, glaring to the mist upon the window. He seemed frozen in time. Slowly, his lips moved. "She was twenty-one. I had just taken my first shift at a foundry. There to keep the property safe from intruders. Our daughter slept peacefully beside her mother." His eyes showed the awful truth of his being there. "I was not there to protect her, when they came, they took everything from me, to take the life of a child is the ultimate sin, but to take the life of a woman, a lady, while carrying the child in her arms, terrified and screaming, takes the most awful of scum, they took me from my duty, to be told my life had ended."

I could not speak; I had caused him such pain in my questioning. "I am so sorry I asked, Jon, I did not know."

"I know, 'twas the reason I joined the sheriffs' men, I couldn't let anyone else suffer what I had suffered, the men who took her started their lives as common thieves, graduating to taking from property, 'twas her screaming that caused them to unleash," he reached forward taking the straw from the bottle, a small drop was all he took that evening. "Francis sentenced them to death, George, the executioner, he said he had taken such great pleasure in taking a life, he was even sure to wrap the rope, so they died slowly, feeling the life leave them, unable to do anything, he's a brutal man, George, but a man of god, and a man who cares for law upon these streets."

"He sounds to be as good as you," I wiped a tear from my eye, "I am here within these chambers to provide pleasant conversation, and here we are speaking of the darkness of this world, the overbearing sadness of a family, lost."

"You do a fine duty, Rose, when I came here, 'twas because of an argument with my sergeant, I considered resigning my duty as a sheriff's man, but you've reminded me of my duty, my reason for putting up with his antics, I do it for her."

"What were their names, Jon?"

He smiled at me, warmly, "Lily and Anna, my wife Lily, she would've liked you, you would've had a good friend in Lily."

"I'm more than sure I would, and now I have a good friend in you."

Jonathan stayed for less than an hour. He left before the light outside dulled, but another visitor to my door soon replaced him. Standing on ceremony, I had changed into a red dress. I know he liked me in red.

"Francis." I took his cloak and helped him sit.

He was silently sat, looking at my face with a warm smile. I felt utterly overwhelmed with sadness. His day had been one of sorrow, saying goodbye to the woman he had known for so long.

"Tell me about her?"

I reached for my bottle. Francis would never partake, he much preferred a sober appearance. "I met her when I was young, my father decided our union would strengthen our family, he was not wrong, but with everything she was, she failed to give me an heir, when my daughter was born father was furious, he was traditional, insisted I needed a male heir, women were too delicate for the harsh world of investment, and he would trust no one marrying into the family, in so many ways, she was lucky she didn't make it, else my father would've destroyed her, Charlotte decided 'twould be best to strengthen the foundation of our house with wealth, she was not wrong, but she was not the one who will now have to live alone."

"It sounds like she had your best interests at heart."

"You can say that now, but I would rather not speak of it. Tomorrow is a new day, and I wish to begin my life as a widower on a positive note. I shall not wander this life alone, Rose."

"Of course not, I will be here waiting for you always."

"Your reason for remaining here is unclear, Rose. That stuff will get you into trouble. 'Tis time you consider removing yourself from such vices."

"Remove myself," I chalked, unaware of his seriousness, "I am sure you only say this to protect me, I am safe here, that is my main reason for staying, I have met honest company and my duty is simple, and the most pleasant duty one could ever wish to have."

"She pushes, Rose," his warning came from nowhere, "eventually, Claudia will ask you for more, most gentlemen want more than pleasant conversation, most want more than a simple chat, the animal who had you, Rose, could be any of those down there, I will always be a friend to you, but the way to keep yourself here, is to dig, find out what your clients really want, provide it, and Claudia will see you well cared for, for the rest of your days."

"I was not planning on staying that long."

"Rose, the romantic notion of you being with a gentleman is one you must now let go, the Lions Chambers or the brothel houses, that is your choice now, they tainted you, no gentleman of good standing would ever consider such a thing."

"Well, I did not expect an insult from you this evening, Francis."

"I do not mean to insult, honesty is always my intention, I am not saying you would not make a good wife, you would make the best wife, I truly believe that, but others would not see it that way, you are a prostitute, Rose, not to give your body, but you give your time, your words and so much more."

It crushed me, such a thing for him to say broke me, I did not consider myself to be one of those women, one of the forgotten, who remained laxed on street corners, laid in filthy beds, 'twas a world I would never explore, I wanted simplicity, I just wanted to be a lady.

Sat by my window, I had my usual view of Holland Street crossing onto Beck Lane, my window cleared by the fogging rain, the smell of fresh rain drifted into the window, the night was dark, clouded, distinct shadows wandered through the streets under the oil lanterns. Dull screams seemed to come from every corner. My eyes drifted towards Beck Lane, a figure emerged from the darkness of High Cross street, the dark figure made his way towards the chambers, passing by, his shadow alone intrigued me, he carried himself well, a striking posture of pride and honesty befell him, the dark clothes made it difficult to see but I could tell he dressed well.

I remained by the window long into the night. The words from Claudia, Francis, and Jonathan they bothered me; I was a lady, and I still intended to become that, regardless of their words, regardless of their jealousies, and regardless of their own vices, I would be a lady one day.

The streets bored me, but sleep was impossible to find. The balcony outside would be empty, void of life but filled with haunting shadows. Against my better judgement, I ventured toward the balcony where a darkness met me. The many doors along the balcony remained the same. I knew there must have been more in there, but I had seen nothing, heard nothing. I was believing I was the only one alongside Claudia. There was once mention of girls within the chambers, but their voices were silent. The balcony guided me toward the stairs, but I passed them by, reaching the other side of the balcony where I came to several more doors, all leading into rooms like mine, apart from one. To the end a large door met me, partially open I could see the long staircase, venturing closer my blood ran cold, the stone stairs made the hairs on my arm stand on end, my foot hit the step with a clacking echo which chased to the top landing. With each step, I felt colder, forcing me to wrap my shoulders with my shawl. The moon lit the walls, silver shadows danced on the walls as I crept up.

Reaching the landing, two rooms sat opposite each other. I reached out, placing my hand on the door. A shuddering fear hit my shoulder. A stiff hand gripped me. Turning, I saw Claudia.

"Not in there," she calmly warned. Turning me from the landing, she guided me back down the stairs, locking the door to the bottom as she did.

"What's up there?" my question was innocent, but it seemed to shake her.

"You will never know, Rose, not unless you wish to live. Stay away from there."

"You said there were more." My language clearly offended her.

"If it is friends you seek, Rose, I am here. You do not need to set out seeking others."

"You said there were others," I insisted with my questioning. "I cannot hear them, to see them. Where are the others?"

She pivoted. "There are no others, Rose," she snapped, "not anymore anyway."

"What happened to them?" my lip quivered; I knew the answer, but I could not bring myself to think of it.

"The Lion's happened, think yourself lucky that they like you, Rose, Moira was too old, they sold her to a brothel in Lincoln, as for Anna, she decided that freedom was something she deserved, and the lions showed her otherwise."

"What did they do to her?"

Her smile twisted. She was just like me, only tainted. She was as animalistic as those men. "She had what was coming to her, the pretty young thing thought she could escape."

"What happened?" again I tried to force an answer from her.

"She's dead!" she scowled, "just like you will be if you venture up those stairs again."

"What is up there, Claudia, I thought I could trust you." I tried to pull her heart.

"Nothing is up there, yet, those are the quarters of the master of the house. Whoever takes the role of John Bentley will receive those quarters."

"Then why are you so insistent I stay away?"

"Because you do not tread where you do not belong, you are still a workhouse girl, a singing one but know your place, Rose, it is not in the quarters of the master."

Her warning was clear, I had overstepped my mark, the boundaries were clear now, if I overstepped again, I would go the way of the others, to a cold hole in the ground, I did not wish to see the end of my days within the chambers, but this would be it for now. I would not be one of the forgotten. I would make a name for myself through my voice. I would become better than Claudia. I would become Rose of Nottingham.

CHAPTER EIGHT A WAY WITH WORDS

I did not intend to become a huntress, my duties continued, my room would always be full of a night-time, client after client. They came and went from my quarters, always with a smile and a promise to return.

The stage would light with my voice, Vivaldi's Gloria, Mozart's soprano arias and solos, Handel, and Bach. I was a marvel upon the stage. When many of them would first meet me, their shock surprised me, shaking hands and sweating brows. Their nerves were often hard to hide, but I would comfort them within my quarters, offering them a vice or two. Adorned with roses, my quarters were like those of a queen or princess. I lived as royalty within the den of iniquity.

Each night I had taken to sitting in the chair, awaiting the shadow to walk by my window, I had taken to following him through to the window in the washroom, trying my best to get a glimpse of his face. His features were masculine, a smooth complexion, neat hair and always so well dressed.

I regret I did not yet know his name; I did not know what his business within the shadows was, or why he walked by my window so often.

A light pressed along my bedroom door, reaching towards me. A shadow in the doorway lingered.

"Is everything alright?" I asked Claudia. She remained at the door.

"I'm well. The chambers were full this evening, and unfortunately, this puts me in a troublesome situation." She rushed in with a letter in her hand, carelessly she threw it at my table.

"What is this?" I asked, wide eyed. I could see the unpleasantness she clearly felt within that letter.

"'Tis from James, James Milner."

"And who is James Milner?"

Harshly she turned, anger filled her face, her eyes widened. "He is the founder of the Lions Chambers Gentleman's Club, along with your precious Francis." Her words spat at me. Her anger confused me. Slowly, I stood from my seat. "He plans to return. Since I sacked off the pustulous fool John Bentley, he feels it is necessary to have a male running the chambers. A woman will not do for him."

She shook with rage. "It has been over a month. You have done a fine job, Claudia. Do not let the venom of a man hinder your work."

"I would say that is kind of you, Rose, but what are we?" her harshness returned. She would hold no regard for my emotion. "I am a whore, nothing more..."

"And nothing less." My calmness intrigued her. "You are a master of men, a manipulator of gentlemen no less, an artisan, bending them to your will." Something came over me, Claudia terrified me when I first arrived, but now, I was her friend, her confident, her apprentice. "You are more than James Milner, Claudia, you are art, and he is nothing but a man."

She instantly calmed. She had seen and felt more than I ever had. She was often the one to calm me, but I was a good apprentice. I had learnt from the best, the most dedicated to the craft of companionship.

She looked to the floor, calming her hurried heart. Her eyes slowly glared at me. "He will want you, you know that?" I shook my head. I did not understand her words. "He will not be happy having a woman here as a companion. Even if you provide your voice upon the stage." Her sneering worried me. Little did I know, all this time, she was protecting me. "No one comes to the Lion and leaves undamaged, Rose, not even you."

"What do you mean?" I felt my mouth draw down, as though my smile was trying to escape my face completely.

"He will want you to work, and there is only one duty for a woman within the chambers. Your voice will not appease him."

My heart quickened. Falling to the chair, I felt disgraced. "Claudia, you wouldn't let him," my eyes burned with pain-filled tears.

Kneeling in front of me, she took my hands in hers. "What choice do I have, in a world run by men?"

"We can leave, both of us?"

"And go where?" she shook her head. She knew sense, but nothing made sense to me anymore. "Rose, you are here now, and there is only one way to escape the chambers, upon the rope of the hangman."

"Then I will tell them all, I will tell them what they do, I will stand in front of judge and jury and speak the truth." I was as quiet as a mouse. It still panicked her.

"Do not speak like that, Rose. Who would believe you? Who would believe the word of a whore, over the word of a judge, a sheriff, men of the law, lords of the highest honours, for the sake of Christ, Rose, we have a knight within these walls, no one would believe you, they would flog and hang you, they would strike your family from history, they have power beyond their means, that is why everything is legal."

I furrowed my brow, confused by her words. "Legal?"

"These streets fill with filth and detritus, 'tis the duty of these men to build a city, leaving the town in the mud where it belongs, but they cannot do that, if they commit murders, Francis knows better than any, if there is a job to be done, the right way is the best way, those who go against the laws of the Lion, they put them to death for crimes they rarely committed, but it makes their death legal and unquestionable, many die so their families can remain safe, Rose, I know you have no family, so if you speak, what do you think they would do to me?"

She was right, she was my family now, as well as Colin who would bring my plate each afternoon, Rosemary, the seamstress, even Robert who would clean the top balcony and the rooms.

"We are truly alone."

She nodded, gently agreeing, "For now we are, Rose, but one day, it may not be like this, we must stay strong."

"And, if I am to do this, you will be safe, I will be safe?"

Her whisper of "yes" soothed me, but as the thought lingered a pain clutched my chest, 'twas the most tincture I had taken in a single evening. I missed my charming gentleman pass that evening, passed out on the bed I remained in a world where I longed to remain. Silken sheets and swirling colours, where everything graced the skin differently, I felt the euphoria swell in me, 'twas my escape. As the morning lingered, I remained in my blissful state.

"Good morning, you." A man's voice called from my door. Shooting from the bed, I covered myself, desperately getting my racing heart to quieten. "I don't mean to barge." He held his hands out. Thick brown brows looked strangely familiar, a black overcoat covered with a dark shadow.

"It's you," my voice croaked, unable to catch my breath.

"Yes, it's me," he was so charming, his smile brightened his face and mine, my gentleman, who I had watched every night, leave his shadows.

He held out his hand to take mine, as a true gentleman would. "Lord Benjamin Connolly," he reached down, kissing the back of my hand. I kept my blue shawl tightly across my front. "My uncle assigned me the duty of caring for the chambers in the absence of a manager."

"Well," I pulled my hand away, wanting to remain brave. "I will have you know Claudia has done a fine duty here. The chambers have never run so smooth."

"As I can tell." He was striking, with a chiselled jawline, piercing brown eyes. Everything about him spoke of perfection. "May I?" he pointed to my chair. Still in shock, I quickly nodded. "She has done a fine duty, however, her other duties prevent her being ever present. We need her elsewhere, and so I lighten her burden."

"Oh, how kind of you," he sensed my sarcasm instantly.

"So, tell me of your duties here, apart from watching me from the window." He gave a wide white smile.

It embarrassed me and he could sense it. "My duty is as an entertainer of an evening, and to provide company, some members here simply wish to have company for the evening."

"And what lovely company they have, but come, what else?"

His question unnerved me, "That is all, I know what these gentlemen want, I know what conversation will please them, but best of all, if it pleases your uncle, they tell me all there is to know of their lives, from the inner workings of their business to what their wife sounds like in the bedroom."

"I thought that was more Claudia's area, so you spend time with them. What else?"

He still pressed with his questions, and I knew I needed to knock him from his pedestal. "If you are asking about the business of Claudia's nature, that being pleasures of the flesh, the answer is no, I am a virgin, and my gentlemen much prefer it that way." I knew 'twas a lie, but I kept my composure, and struck him down. "Lord Connolly..."

"Please, it's Ben."

"Very well, Ben, I do not partake in such vulgarities, and not all men wish to either," he sniggered at my comment. "Well, if you think it so amusing, ask yourself this, what better draw to return to the chambers, than to see a lady untouched, to be tempted by such overwhelming need it drags you back night after night, I am Rose of Nottingham, the untouched whore, the soprano of Goose Gate, 'tis what kept you wandering by my window, knowing you would never taste the forbidden fruit, knowing, 'tis what keeps them returning, night after night, they pay to sit with me, some will take with me, others simply long for my company, I am good at my duty, Lord Connelly, and I will have no inexperienced overseer tell me different, I know your uncles chambers, I know what the lions want of me."

"Usually a pound of flesh," he commented as he stood. I could feel him melt with my words. "But I see your point, Rose," he slowly left towards the door, turning to look at me over his shoulder. "You know, I don't know why I walked by your window each night, I easily could've gone a different way, but you must have enchanted me, just as you have the gentlemen here, who knew, they live among us." He smirked as he left my room. I had beaten him, for now.

I would need to defend my virginity. As soon as Ben discovered the truth, he would put me to the lions, just as Claudia was, and all those before me. I knew nothing of those before me, and I cared little, 'twas about me now, keeping myself safe and untainted for as long as I could.

The dawn brought a cloudy day, the scent of petals filled the spring air, blossom on the breeze had me clawing at the window, longing to be there, upon the banks of the river in Sutton, where the bluebells grew among long grasses, where snowdrops and buttercups lived peacefully side by side, I longed to feel the cold air from the river upon my skin again, the warm embrace of the summer sun as it poured to the spring fields surrounding. I never thought the day would come, but I deeply missed the workhouse. I missed the stench, the sound of screaming children, the blood curdling squeal of a child being punished by one of the sisters. No one could punish quite like a nun.

I had taken worse beatings than the one the chambers had given, but I knew, with the arrival of Benjamin Connolly, the chambers were about to feel his darkness.

I admired him for his looks. The beauty of a man had never stricken me before until Ben came. My days soon turned from loneliness to fulfilled bliss. He visited me each afternoon before the chambers opened its doors. I always felt his warm eyes inspect me.

"I understand now," he commented, holding a small glass of golden spirit. Gracefully, I turned. "I see the appeal."

"Well, there isn't much to see, Ben. I'm positively charming," wobbling my head I amused him.

"You are, Rose, but there is something else," his smile withered. "You are now reaching eighteen, at the end of the year I believe, and yet, you remain with a childlike charm, something about you, Rose, you would pass as a small innocent girl, were it not for your height," he sniggered.

"I'm not that childlike, they hear me sing as any Italian soprano, worthy of the title of lady." I tried to defend myself, unaware of the face he saw within me. "I am a woman, a lady no less."

"You are a lady, Rose, but truly, these men are after a fine quality of woman, lady, I mean, and they have that with you, because you remind them of their childhood romances, the daughter they never had, the granddaughter they long to meet, you remind them of the innocence of youth."

"Perhaps, but there is nothing sinister in their desires."

"Not that you know of, that's simply because of where you are," he leant forward, whispering, "you believe you know men, you know little of the men I know, Rose, they are not all gentle."

"Well, if you are so sure, why would you allow such iniquitous behaviour within these walls?"

"Tripping me up won't work. They have not acted inappropriately. However, what goes on in their heads, that's a different story."

I laughed at his comment. "So come on then, Ben, what were you doing all those nights? When you emerged from the shadows."

He glared at me. A darkness in his eyes frightened me. His lips parted, not wanting to speak. "As I say, if you knew, you would understand, not all gentlemen are gentle." I sat back, concerned by his words. "Worry not, my flower, you are safe, you're the property of my uncle, even I'm not stupid enough to damage that."

His sniggering enraged me. "I am no one's property."

"If you say so, flower."

"I do say so, and I mean it, I belong to no man!"

He slowly stood from the chair, "Ah, and there was you, insisting that one day you would be a lady, didn't you know, Rose, to be a lady means you give yourself to a gentleman, you are property, Rose, whether in these chambers or not, you do not belong to yourself, flower, you belong to men."

That was his view, and it sickened me, I was no property, I was not to be traded, he left my room as quickly as he came, I knew he brought darkness with him, but the shadows within the chambers were becoming darker. Since his arrival, I had barely glanced at Claudia. Always in her quarters, the staff cleaned with their heads down low. Even the streets outside seemed too frightened to make too much noise. He had come with a purpose, and now that purpose was being fulfilled, I feared what else Benjamin had in mind for the chambers.

"Do you wish to take a day out tomorrow?" asked Claudia, stood behind me she helped brush my hair. She seemed to enjoy our time together.

"I fear I wouldn't return, Benjamin. He simply seems different to John."

She stood straight, looking at my reflection in the mirror. "I know. I am regretting my actions. However, he simply needs time to settle, he feels a need to assert his dominance as many men do, and he will leave us to our tasks."

"Our tasks," I whispered, I looked to the dresser in front, everything was so lavish, but I was nothing but a stage diva, 'twas all an act, all for show, I had no feelings for that place since Benjamin had arrived, my gentleman of the darkness had a side I did not wish to see.

"That is what this is, Rose, your task, your duty, if you wish for the chambers to be anything more, then only you can change that, I enjoy my duty now, I didn't use to, you once told me we have the power to manipulate, use that power on Benjamin," she paused for a moment, a calling from the street outside distracted us both.

The voices muffled, angry shouting. I could hear the most despicable threats of death coming towards the chambers, followed by a call.

"I doubt it, John. Take yourself away and calm yourself. A week of banishment should see you fit." The voice sounded like Benjamin. I joined Claudia by the window. It looked out onto Goose Gate, where we saw Benjamin standing in the road. Several horses passed by with their master's wares toward the large market in the centre of the town. Stepping to one side, Benjamin looked to the window where he saw us peering towards him.

Claudia and I shot back, feeling our hearts race as we ran towards the balcony. Seeing him storm inside, he looked at the both of us, mouths gaping.

"Now is your chance," whispered Claudia. She raised her brows at me.

I knew my duty, but 'twas about to change. I hurried down the stairs and into the bar. Usually I would not leave my room, given my duty was to stay.

"Are you alright?" panic struck my voice, Benjamin calmed.

His smile tightened towards me, "Back to your room, the doors will open soon."

"I would, but I first need to be sure you are well."

"I'm fine, Rose, thank you for your concern, however we all have a duty here. Yours is in your room."

"Come with me," I was soft for Benjamin, something about him told me of a childlike madness he missed in his youth, they raised him in silence, never allowed to laugh too loud, never allowed to play or form friendships, 'twas a sad life of privilege.

"Come with you where?"

His squint at first concerned me. "You're shaking, Ben. You need to calm before anyone else arrives. Please, come with me and calm yourself."

He looked to the balcony where Claudia still stood. She gave a nod to Benjamin before retiring to her quarters. Following me up the stairs, I had Benjamin caught in my web, he was mine to manipulate, but I needed to tread carefully, he was not like the others, he saw past the smoke and mirrors of common conversation, what he required was much deeper.

The sun had warmed the room, but still I caught a server on my way to have a fire lit. He sat silently, waiting for me to lead him.

"I just needed to be sure you were well." I stood by the door, waiting for the server to bring a drink for Benjamin. "Your duties here are difficult, Ben."

"I'm aware of that, Rose, I just don't understand some people." He opened to me completely. I passed his glass to him, lowering into the seat opposite. I intended to listen to everything. "John bloody Corn, he's insane, yet he still makes a fortune in the foundries. How can a man of such poor talent have gained such prestige?" he looked towards me, expecting an answer.

"What is it he wanted?"

Shaking his head, he took a sip before he replied, "He wished to ask our members for investment, it's simple manners, you wait for investment offers, you do not ask for it, and his mannerisms, he practically demanded investment from our members."

"Passion," I sniggered. "That's all it is, Ben. He has passion, a belief in his investment, but without your help his dream will wither and die."

He glared at me. "Why should I help a man realise his dream, when so many have theirs crushed each day?"

"Well, now we speak of dreams. Surely you aren't a man to crush them?"

"I am a man to realise my own dreams. It takes effort, hard work, and dedication. John Corn has none of those. His foundries have failed because of his lack of management."

"What was his proposal?" My question seemed to shift his eyes closer to me. Doubt spilled from them. "Of course I don't mean to invest." My laughter did not amuse him.

"Good, it would be a hopeless investment, he plans on a new water tower, close to the Leen, also one in the Trent, to clean the waters, the smell from the Leen is becoming unbearable I can't deny, but his plans are simple, too simple, he is an eccentric, and now his parents are dead he expects everyone else to invest as they did."

"It sounds sad," lowering my head I felt sympathy for John Corn. He did not seem like the type of person who should've wandered the streets alone. "Perhaps the grief of losing his parents has triggered a madness in him?"

"And he can take it elsewhere. I do not wish to entertain his idiosyncrasies."

I leant forward, using what womanly charm I had I placed my hand on his lap. "Do you feel better now?"

His smile grew towards me, a softness in his eyes invited me. "Much better, thank you, Rose, for actually caring."

"That is what I do," I sat back feeling melancholy, I missed the old me, the young girl who cared far too much, since finding out about Gladys and Tom my loyalty had changed somewhat, I belonged to Claudia now, and the Chambers, which meant my loyalty was now with Ben.

"What is it?"

"I'm fine," I replied unsurely. He sat forward, knowing I was lying. "It is my duty here to listen. My problems are my own." My smile remained; I hid my feelings well until now.

"When my uncle sent me here, I thought my duty and talents wasted, I have managed much bigger than this, but he insisted, he has no male heir, and so he believed it best I took over, and that makes me your caretaker, and if something is amiss, I need to know."

"Nothing is amiss, Ben, everything is perfect." I was trying to be honest. I appreciated my caregivers. I had a warm bed, much more than those in Leen Side. The houses were cheap there for a reason. They fed me, never hungry, never wanting more.

"I sense you had a dream once," his soft voice deepened, drawing me closer.

Bashfully I smiled, "I did, and now I suppose that dream is somewhat of a reality, for a girl like me at least."

"Tell me."

His request concerned me. What would he think of a simple girl from a workhouse who prayed to be a lady, to marry a gentleman.

"I had dreamt of marriage once, to a gentleman of excellent reputation, that's all gone now."

"Because you know?"

"I know, real gentlemen, Ben, they are not always what we expect, I have met very few since being here, 'tis my duty to entertain them, and although I am not Claudia I am worse, you were right, and Claudia, I whore myself on a much worse level, she gives her body, I give my mind, my soul, my everything, all while knowing I will never have my own family, I lied to myself for so long, believing I could still have that, the truth is, I will never have that, my dream died the day I came to Nottingham."

"Very deep, Rose, but perhaps, you are one of the lucky ones, most ladies have to put up with the same one, night after night, the same gentleman coming to their quarters, the same complaints and aging bones, greying hair, and skin, at least you can have a different one by the hour."

"One way of putting it, but I don't want this forever. Now I know I have no choice. This is me now, the Rose of Nottingham, there to entertain, to provide a getaway from the burden of title."

"Well, I have no title, but you provide me that getaway," he was tender. A flirtation came from him, and I invited it, pursing my lips as I leant forward. "I struggled at first to understand why they would employ such an ordinary girl, not for the duties of lying, but for a duty as simple as singing and talking. I realise now, your company is charming."

He stood, making his way slowly towards the door. "Then perhaps I can include you on my list?"

He had such a sweet smile, "I would rather be on a different list, a list of friends perhaps."

"That sounds wonderful." I watched him leave. I was there to enchant people, to help them drift away from their hard day, but he had enchanted me. He had come from the shadows, and brought light into a life so dismal. My loyalties to the chambers strengthened. The charms of Benjamin caught me.

CHAPTER NINE LADY LILY

I had a surprise for Ben, rousing the crowd with an additional orchestra, I had also hired several singers, both male and female, to join me that evening upon the stage, where a rendition of Mozart's Dies Irae blew the roof off the Chambers. Followed by my attempt to welcome Ben to the chambers, I had noticed his hint of Yorkshire accent within, forcing my research into local songs, the only one I could find of pleasant note was 'On Ilkla Moor Baht 'at,' he laughed at the bar with my rendition, I believed it was an enjoyable evening for all, until I came to leave the stage, having my arm caught as I left, I looked to Ben.

"Don't do that again," he warned.

"I simply wished to welcome my friend." I was unsure of his temper.

"I appreciate the sentiment, Rose, but never do that again. The stage remains as yours and yours alone."

Deflated, I left towards my quarters, ready to receive my gentlemen for the evening.

I regretted upsetting Ben. I had planned a pleasant evening for him, helping him settle into the chambers. He was my friend now. Each day he would visit me, he knew I was still as pure as the day I arrived at the chambers. Benjamin had become closer than Francis to me. Claudia had remained away, always busy, always with someone new. I struggled to understand how she enjoyed her duty, giving herself to different men each night. The very thought made my skin crawl.

Seeing another winter in the chambers at first seemed daunting, but now it seemed to open me to hope. The world was colder than usual. A harsh winter approached. The chambers would be busy over the winter. I had noticed a larger gathering than usual. Although I would return to my room following my show, I sneaked a few glances when another client would enter.

The bitterness of winter was biting at my window, but I welcomed it. Sitting in my quarters day after day was picking at my spirit. I had all I needed, but even my vice didn't seem to calm me anymore. Everything I did was for the sake of the chambers now, but that was all about to change.

"What are your dreams now, Rose?" asked Francis. His nightly visit always warmed my room.

"My dreams have not changed, Francis. I still wish to one day find the gentleman I can call my own."

He sniggered, looking at the glass he cupped in his hand. "Well, it looks like you may have found one," his eyes lingered towards me, "Benjamin never stops staring at your door."

His voice carried an inquisitive wonder, "He is my friend, my manager no less," it was ridiculous to think of Benjamin in that way, "we have become close, but friendship is all we will ever have, he is a real gentleman, a lord no less..."

"You search for gentlemen and when you find one you see yourself as unworthy," he chuckled at me, ponderously I sat beside him. "Tell me of your parents."

His question surprised me. We had spoken before of my upbringing, but never so far back to mention my parents. "I know very little. I was young when they died. I did not know of them."

"What were their names? Their work?"

He was truly inquisitive, 'twas a side I always enjoyed seeing, but he pushed for an answer. "I don't know their work, but I know their names, Lily and Graham Stoke," he widened his eyes, as if caught by a moment of thought. "What is it?"

"Nothing, it's just, nothing." His hesitation had me worried.

"Please, Francis, if you knew them I wish to know all I can..."

"No, I did not know them. Besides, they're gone now. What good would that do?" he was harsh, his tone changed, "bring me a drink."

I stood, my lips still parted with surprise. His reaction completely took me aback. If he knew my parents, why would he find a need to lie to me.

Nights seemed to go on forever. Most of my visits would comprise my vice being overused by those who saw it as their pleasure. To them 'twas no vice. I spent most days exhausted, my mind often wandered, food became ash in my mouth, water did not seem to quench my thirst, I did not care for the pleasure of company anymore, I was withdrawing from the world, and I knew it.

"Good morning," Claudia greeted me in my chambers. Making her way in, I noticed a shadow on her face. A yellow bruise was still healing.

"What happened to you?" I hurried towards her, seeing her face closer.

She turned her head from me,
"Nothing," her spirit seemed to have withered,
"nothing for you to concern yourself with."

She slowly sat at the window table. A
warm spring sun danced in the room, a calling of
birds drifted in on the cool breeze.

"Surely it was something, Claudia. I
haven't seen a glimpse of you in an age. What
happened?"

"A mishap of duties, that's all," her
withering smile showed a deeper pain within.

"Claudia, tell me?" I was abrupt. She
needed to know I would always be there for her
as a friend and guide.

"Rose," her eyes softened towards me, an
eerie feeling hit the room, causing my skin to
grow cold and bump. "The chambers are
changing."

"What change," the thought amused me,
"I've seen no change."

"Because you spend your night
completely disconnected, Rose. From the stage
you arrive back here and... that stuff, it has you in
its clutches..."

"Not that bad." My argument was invalid
and even I felt it. "I have to, 'tis what they
demand of me, 'tis my reason for being here,
talking to them and taking with them, were it not
for me this place would fail..."

"It is failing, Rose, and we need to find a way to keep them coming, the town is growing but the chambers are shrinking, Benjamin has put forward a proposal, he wishes to keep you as you are, but I am the only lady of the night the chambers have, he has tasked me the duty of employing other ladies, however, he has tasked you the duty of finding out what our patrons want, you have not been doing your duty, Rose, you need to tell him by the end of the week, their deepest and darkest desires, Benjamin is a coward, he would ask you himself but fear reprisal..."

"What are you saying?" I could sense something more.

"The streets are cold, all year round, Rose, if you do not comply with his wishes, 'tis where you will be, and the lions will not see you upon the streets of Nottingham, the gallows await those who do not comply with the Lions."

Her words frightened and confused me. She spoke of Ben as a monster. "What are you talking about?"

"It's business, Rose, I know you like Benjamin, but he is your caretaker, and if you do not provide what he wants, he will dispose of you as he sees fit, you are property, Rose, that's all, he is not your friend." Her warning hit me hard. She was being serious. A fear in her voice forced me to listen. Her fear terrified me. The bruises on her face told me I needed to listen in order to survive.

"I need more tincture," my cowardly voice whimpered.

"I will get you all you need, so long as you provide for the lions."

"I will do all they require of me."

"Then ask them, find their deepest and darkest secrets, their innermost desires. You are the only one they'll tell, Rose."

That evening was cold in the light of the spring moon. A frosty glare towards my visitors seemed to unnerve them. I soon broke from the conversation I'd had with Claudia and returned to my business.

Placing a single drop of tincture into the mouth of Mark I settled beside him, he was a strange fellow, young, barely out of his teens, but he knew his wants, forced to grow too fast by his overbearing father who'd died of an illness a few years before, I was his only escape from the depression of the real world he faced.

"Tell me your deepest, darkest secrets," my whisper into his ear made him shudder, "your innermost desires."

He drifted for a while, deep within the world I had created for him, unable to close his lips properly even. He was in ecstasy. His eyes flickered, leaving the world I gave him as he drifted for a while between worlds. He soon loosened to me.

"I have it here, Rose."

It flattered me, but I knew he was holding back, "Come on, Mark, tell me, what it is you desire the most, be it family, career, love?" I ran my finger around the outside of his ear, knowing it made him shudder and loosen further.

"My darkest secrets are my own, Rose, I cannot say."

"They will not leave this room. All I can do, is try to make them real. You are between worlds, Mark. Now is the time to find yourself. Be honest with yourself, no one else will." His shoulders relaxed. He looked at the table, unsure. "You can trust me, Mark. When have I ever let you down?"

His flickering brow came with promise. "I suppose, my deepest desires may sicken you, Rose. You would never look at me the same way again. You would look to me as a monster..."

"Never," I reached forward, trying to reassure him, trying to keep him talking.

"They frown upon my desires, but 'twas a practice we all seemed to indulge in not too long ago, even now, in some areas."

He saw my look of confusion, a furrowed brow and curled lip. "I like women, Rose, but my father never allowed me a childhood, I simply desire that, a chance to find what my friends all did, a chance to experience my first kiss, without me having to pay a monthly fee for it, a chance to relive my youth, in a single night." My blood ran cold. He did not need to speak any more, even so, he did. "I like girls, Rose, not women. Their experience often frightens me. They know men, and I would like to teach someone, in a single night, just to feel what my younger self missed."

I was not expecting such a reply. His callous mind had thoughts of young girls, taking their innocence just as they took mine, 'twas his passion, his need to remove the innocent.

The night lingered with no joy, something sucked from the room, my mind wandered more that evening than any before, sat by my window I had felt strange, I no longer desired the outside world, it frightened me, so many passed my quarters, but I thought I knew nothing about them, in all honesty, I had neglected my innermost thoughts, taking each man who came to my chambers as a gentleman with a slight need to relax with the help of my tincture, I already knew all I needed to know about them, all their vices, their secrets, their lies.

"How was this evening for you?" Benjamin stood by my door, slowly ambling in, squirming like the worm he was.

"'Twas a strange evening," my voice muffled, having my hand pressed on my lips, eyes wide in contemplation towards the window.

"Well, what can you tell me?"

He reached towards me, placing his dirty hand on my lap. I quickly removed it. "I am not yours to touch, Ben," he sensed my mood. Even I did not know what had adjusted my temperament so much.

He sat back, crossing one leg over the other, but not before reaching for the bottle on the table. Taking a single drop, he sat back, still within this world, but not without relaxation.

"I can tell you more than you need to know, Ben, but this comes at a cost." Gauging his reaction, he did not move. "I know more than you will ever know of these men, but everything I tell you remains in this room."

"Not going to happen," he mumbled, breaking from his trance. "Rose, the chambers are failing, we need income, which means we need to keep bringing more, by showing our patrons we will do anything to please them, we will bring all we need to, now, unless you wish to wander a dark, cold street for the rest of your days, always looking over your shoulder," he leant forward, reading my eyes, "Do you think you're the first, Rose?" his smug grin disheartened me, he sang the words, "there once was a girl called Betty, who's voice made you shake like a jetty, with a blink of the eye, she said her goodbye now Betty walks alone unpretty. They threw her from the chambers, unable to comply. She joined a brothel on Fisher Gate, and when she saw what monsters we were, she turned to theft. They hanged two weeks before they took you on here."

My heart fluttered, a lump in my throat forced the words from my chest. "Francis desires nothing but company, Colin Spring, he is a man of many desires, it's doubtful you could fulfil them all, John Burridge, he likes older, more mature women, someone who can and will take charge, he likes pain, I once burned him with candle wax, his smile unnerved me, then there's Stephen Thorn, his desire lies with the darkest, like you..." his brows raised and lips parted, "Children."

My mistake came when I told him that not only did he now know everything of his innocent patrons, but he also now knew he was not alone.

"Thank you, Rose, you are an asset to the chambers, in more ways than one."

I set my sentence that day. I never quite realised how low one would fall just to see their own success.

CHAPTER TEN NEVER A LADY

The road outside was the furthest I dare go, the bins to the side of me rattled. Believing it could've been a cat or stray dog, I ignored it, until another rattle threw the lid from the bin. Gasping in fright, I stood back. A small boy with dirty blond hair and tattered clothes looked at me, a creature from a bin. His smile was wide and pleased to see me.

"Good morning," I greeted.

"Morning, Ma'am," he called to me, holding a pitiful lump of discarded bread.

"What are you doing?"

"Eating, ma'am, it's amazing what this place chucks."

I furrowed my brows, stepping forward. "Where are your parents?"

"Don't have none," he replied with little care or feeling.

"Your workhouse then?"

The boy scoffed. "Please, I ain't that daft, avoid them like the plague."

The boy seemed smart, but rummaging around in bins was not my idea of a pleasant situation.

"Well, you can't eat that."

He took a hearty bite. "Why not?"

"It's not very nice," I chuckled, "look, what's your name?"

"William, but my friends call me Billy."

"Alright, hopefully I can call you Billy. Would you like to come inside, I see can about getting you something proper to eat."

His mouth gaped, dropping the bread from his hand as he crawled from the bin. His excitement carried him towards the door.

"Ain't this the chambers? Where the judge and that is?" he was fearful of that place, I could not blame him.

"It is, but they aren't all bad in here. I live here, and I'm rather friendly." I tried to keep a warm smile towards him, hoping he would not run with fright.

"You live here? You a prostitute or something?"

"Not exactly, I'm a singer..."

He turned to the front of me, "You're Rose, that lady who sings. We all hear it out here. I can't believe it's you." Crouching in front, his awe shocked me. "I hear you every night.

Sometimes I close my eyes and pretend to be in there."

"Really?"

He quickly nodded, escorting him towards the back. Ben gave an awful glare. He thundered towards me.

"Please calm down," I insisted, holding my hands up. "He is hungry, that's all."

"A moment, Rose," he pulled me to one side. I could feel his anger boiling from him. "If we invite one, they'll all start turning up, Rose. What did you think you were doing?"

"Helping an innocent child down on his luck, he has no parents, not even a workhouse, Ben. We have to help him."

"We do not have to do anything of the sort..."

I spoke with a hushed tone. "Perhaps some work here, he would earn his keep, we always have leaks from the gutters, the birds drop some awful things within the gutters, before you know it these rooms will flood, and then we have the sweeps, we wouldn't need them if we had our own." I pleaded with him. Something about that boy spoke to me. I knew he would be a worthy worker. "Please, Ben, give him a chance."

Ben glared at me. A look into my begging eyes softened him. "Are you willing to work, boy?" he asked, turning towards Billy.

"Billy, sir, my friends call me Billy, and I would work. I'd do anyfin now, anyfin to get a dry roof."

"Well, if you can show me you're willing to work, then the dry roof is yours." Ben quickly turned, calling as loud as he could, "Marcus!" He looked back to Billy. "You'll be the apprentice of Marcus. He deals with maintaining the building, listen to every word he says, one foot wrong and you will be back on the streets, boy."

"Yes, sir, I'll do my best I always do."

"That's not promising, considering where you came from." Ben glared back towards me, "You're trouble, Rose, do you know that."

I curtsied towards him, flirting with his inability to say no to me.

Weeks lingered, and I gave Ben all he wanted of me. Every secret, every lie, every skeleton in their closets were now in the hands of Benjamin. I was my worst enemy; forced to do nothing. I could've lied, but I found myself in a hard situation. I did not wish to starve on the streets, or see myself hanged for steeling bread. I made my decision and now I needed to stick with it. As much as I hated myself, I was weak.

'Twas a dirty addiction, most of those within the brothels had the same habit, their vices were the same as mine, although, I had never taken to drinking the ruin, I was in two minds, the tincture was what got me here, along with the help of Gladys and Tom, but I could no longer blame them, the rooms to the upper chambers had sat empty, apart from the rooms of the staff, but the empty rooms would soon fill, with the abomination which would cost me my everything.

The storm had come to the town of Nottingham, and I was the one who invited it there. Those rooms filled with a sight I never wanted to see, girls as young as thirteen, not everyone knew about those rooms, and I couldn't tell anyone, 'twas a secret I swore to keep, a secret I did not want.

I had seen Billy a few times. I would smile at him outside my window when he would wash them during the day. Being hung over by Marcus Pickle, the maintenance of the building was an ongoing burden to them. Billy seemed happy there. His spirit shone as he continued his duty within the chambers.

Sporting a fresh black eye, Claudia glared towards me over the balcony. I knew it was him. Ben was rough. He liked it that way, and Claudia was the only one there to take what he offered.

"What?" I mouthed the word and shrugged. She lifted her upper lip, returning to her room, looking to the floor below. Ben looked at me. His look was different. He looked at me with love, kindness.

"A moment, Rose," he called. I retreated to my room, awaiting his arrival.

"You've done well, Rose," bursting into my door, he saw my look of hate and fury.

"I have done despicable things, Ben. Nothing that happens here is good, not anymore..."

"It never was, Rose," he raised his voice. Slowly he came towards me, holding my wrists as his grip tightened. "Do you get it now, Rose, you belong to me, to the chambers. You belong to us all. The lions always get what we want."

"The girl I saw, she is a child," I tried to shout, but my weakened body wouldn't allow me. "Just a child, Ben."

"We were all children once. What makes her so different?"

It disgusted me. Never had I thought I would hear such a thing. "What happened to you?"

"That isn't your business," he snapped, throwing my wrists from his hands I felt the blood rush back into my arms. "This place has taken me." Reptilian rage filled his eyes, an animalistic tone spilt from him. "I came here to fix this place, to make it better, only to find it was being run by two whores who fancied their way with business," he hissed at me. He hated me. "You're a temptress, Rose, and a good one, I'll give you that," sweat covered his brow. I had never seen such a mood hit him.

"Ben, please calm down," I shook and begged, wanting him to stop, the chambers were quiet downstairs, the only ones left would've been the night porter, tucked deep in his room toward the back of the building, Claudia did not try to come to my rescue, as soon as I said those words, he snapped, like a twig in a winter wood his mind was no longer his own, his violation of me cut deeper than any knife, for the second time in my young life, I realised I was never a lady, and I would never be one.

"Ben, please, no!" I called out, but no one would listen, he was teaching me a lesson, I had teased them all, I had shown them what they desired and could never have, but Ben was the king of the lions, he would take what he wanted, I was his to do with as he pleased, his plaything, I was nothing to him and he needed to show me exactly that.

"How will you face him?" Claudia stood bitterly in my chambers the next morning, a green shawl covered the bruises on her shoulders.

"I don't know, I don't want to face him, ever again, I just want to go."

"You can't do that, Rose, you know that." I heard the sympathy in her voice, and now I knew her resentment of me.

"He did it to you, didn't he?" I was not angry with her, I was not cruel, I was Rose, the understanding child of the chambers, the more I had thought with a sober mind, the more I realised, this was no longer my home, 'twas my final resting place.

"What happens, Claudia? What happens when we are too old, when we are grey and old, when our bodies have withered?"

"You don't need to worry about that, Rose," a glisten of a tear fell from her eye. "You'll be dead long before that happens."

"What?" a surge of shock snapped through me, "dead?"

"Rose, when you first started taking your medicine, what did the pharmacist say?" her question seemed strange.

"I wasn't there."

"Exactly, you all get sent here, to us, or the taverns, Gladys and Tom, they have a working system, they take in young girls, give them a vice, and exploit it, just like they did you, Betty's vice was alcohol, her habit got her killed, and yours will do the same..."

"Then what is yours?"

"Mine," her smile widened with a maddened grin, "Men, they are my vice, I enjoy men, their cruelty, their gentleness, their touch, their smell, everything."

She was not the same as me. What he did had sickened me, all the threats, all the hate that he had thrown at me. I needed to get out with my life intact, before they could end it for me. My plan was not clear, my head shaded from my addiction, I could not think without it, but with it, I could not run, that bottle, 'twas the chain around my neck, I needed it to survive, but it would become my death.

The murmurs from the rooms along the balcony paled as the evening drew on. Carl, my concierge by my door, gave me my list of appointments for that evening. The first on my list was Francis, a delight after such an awful day.

Claudia burst into the room, giving an unexpected fright. She slammed the door behind her, grabbing my arm as she hurriedly sat me down.

"What is it?" I saw the fear of a thousand storms in her eyes, the same fear we would give when a bolt of lightening would hit the tower in the workhouse.

"You can say nothing," she begged. She rocked as she spoke. "Rose, please, you can say nothing to Francis of this."

"Of what?"

"Of Ben, if Francis found out you would see a side to these gentlemen you would never wish to see, they will defend this place with their lives, with everything, please, Rose, promise me."

Quickly, I nodded. She had lost her mind. A dishevelled look was not befitting her. She usually held a calm demeanour, never so shaken, but something had frightened her.

"Claudia, what did he tell you?"

Her eyes softened. She sat straight. I felt terrified of her once, but now, she was weak, she had lost all power. "Do you ever ask yourself, why you?" she looked at me with a look I had missed, a look of longing, a look of love. "This isn't the first time the chambers manager has felt threatened by a need to better the chambers, Rose, it happened to John as well..."

"John Bentley?"

"He was in a predicament, being asked constantly to fill the rooms, but he did not see sense in increasing the trade I do, the men here, they are gentlemen, they could find a brothel on Fisher Gate, why sully the chambers as well, and so, he asked his confidant, Francis, he had seen a lost girl within the town, he called you enchanting, said you had the smile of a dazzling sun, he could've talked to you for hours, but he mentioned your vice, said you would be safer here and provide a different company for those who wish to partake."

"He is a magistrate, and as such, he does not partake in such vices, but why me?"

"He would be ashamed to admit it, his sister," her hesitation worried me. There was more to Francis than I had first realised. "'Tis not my place. The next time he is here, ask him about his family, but not his wife. Ask him of his brothers and sisters."

"Why?"

"You may just realise you are not here by chance or fate," she slowly stood. She knew my belief in fate, my desire to find mine. "It isn't real, Rose, fate. It is a fantasy you would be best to let go of. Hope, Rose, it hurts."

I knew Claudia had suffered, but how deep it went was yet to be seen. Her suffering lived in her eyes. Each time she spoke of her duty in the chambers, I struggled to understand her dedication, but my addiction had brought me such dedication, without the chambers, I would suffer and waste, like those on Fisher Gate.

The weeks passed; a soft summer was welcome that year, but as the months drew closer to winter, the bitterness returned to the chambers. Leaving for my morning commute I passed Carlton Street and onto Pelham Street, trying my best to miss the Weekday, I avoided that place now for fear of seeing Tom with his batches of cockles, or Gladys calling to the crowd of her wares, upon seeing Mr Stafford in the market square, who would usually help his father selling cockles, I lowered my head and passed quickly, I had shame in that town now, the chambers were the only place where I felt safe, out here, upon the mighty streets of Nottingham, I felt small, the world was watching me, judging me, I had avoided all, using my tincture to escape the reality of the failing world, I never expected, at twenty, how bitter my life could become.

I did not know my purpose that day, I simply walked, not wanting to return to the chambers, I passed many that morning, some looked to me with judging eyes and others with a welcome smile, I dressed like a lady, but deep down my hope withered, knowing I was never a lady and never would be.

A large street faced me. I did not know how far I had wandered. I simply walked. The streets were slowly settling into darkness. Turning back, I saw fate was real. It faced me in a window of a small derelict looking house. A woman stood, a face full of tears, ripped dress and red sores on her body, a man left the house through a door to the side, I peered down, frightful he might see me, he kept on his merry way, tilting his hat to the people on the busy streets.

Rushing toward the house, I frantically hammered at the door, stood dishevelled in the doorway. A look of angered shock caught her face.

"I apologise. I saw you from the window. Are you alright?"

She saw my concern but brushed it off as a simple case of nosiness. "I'm fine, love, and you, make a habit of looking in people window's, do you?"

Her snapping tone had me unnerved. "No, certainly not, but I couldn't help but notice..."

"Away with you love, they get handsie round here, that's all, a bit of a slap about every so often, can be good for the spirit..."

"But that man hurt you," my argument was invalid. She invited it.

"He paid well to see me suffer. 'Swat we do to survive. I don't ask you about your business, so don't you be asking me of mine. Now, I'll thank you to leave."

"I apologise, I simply wanted to be sure you were safe." My explaining did no good, it only seemed to anger her more.

Turning towards me, her mouth gaped, "Oi, one minute, aren't you that Rose?"

"That's my name." I was astonished. I had never seen this woman, but she seemed to know me. "How do you know?"

"This world ain't as innocent as you believe, lovey, we all have things in common, I do what I do to survive, at least I didn't sell my soul to the devil, they can still welcome me in a church."

"I don't know who you think I am, but you are very much mistaken..."

"I don't make mistakes in the whoring world. Circles talk, and they talk all the time about the Rose of Nottingham. Your body isn't what they want, it's your voice and mind."

"I'm an entertainer. I simply talk to these men, gentlemen actually, and I have never whored myself. I simply provide company, nothing more and nothing less."

"Then ask yourself this, what do you give to them they don't already have, and what do you take from them that is so dangerous, because their ain't no point without danger, you're at the chambers, aren't you?"

"That's where I live."

"Where you'll die more like, so many before you, as soon as you become a waste, they'll get rid and a new bright beaming rose will replace you, you're nothing to them."

She left into the house, leaving me flummoxed on the street, I did not know what I had done to offend this woman, or what the chambers had done to cause such unrest, I did not want to return, but I had little choice.

CHAPTER ELEVEN HOW WINTER CAME

The cold grasps of winter came and went, my days drifted into nights, the chambers were my cell, the servers my gaolers, my duty was as perfect as it could be, I did not know happiness anymore, not without my tincture, and I would do anything to ensure my bottle remained full.

I passed everything I was told by my clients to Benjamin. The spirit of Billy was withering. I would still see him, but more and more I would see the dwindling of his spirit. Something in that place was evil, but I failed to see what. My eyes were weary, my sight had faded, time and my addiction were getting the better of me, I had a duty to the chambers, I no longer mattered.

My concern for Billy grew. Seeing him less and less unnerved me. I had spoken to Claudia. Seeing her on the balcony brought shameful tears to my eyes. I saw the pain she suffered, but speaking of Billy seemed to heighten that pain. Even Benjamin would not speak of it. Until the day I did not see Billy, days passed and still no sign of him. My asking of his whereabouts always met with the same shrugging shoulders and blank expression.

Night-time's in the chambers were always silent, the streets outside were lit with the dull flicker of oil lanterns, never reaching to the windows of the chambers. The moon that night was absent, as was my sleep. Silently, I crept from my quarters and to the balcony. The shadows were overwhelming to the sight, so using my other senses, I could hear the dull moans from the streets outside. A horse neighed in the distance. But the cold chambers were still silent. Making my way toward the end of the balcony, something pulled me. The master's quarters were a place they had warned me away from before, but now I felt drawn to them, I could use the excuse I wished to see Ben, the frightening night wanted me to seek comfort in his company, I hated him for what he had done to me, but he had woken me to my true self.

The steps were cold as I climbed upwards. The open landing was lit by a single flame from a small lantern on the wall beside the master's chambers. That was not the door I wished to open, to the left, another door stood lonely in the night, silence behind the door was terrifying, creeping slowly towards it I hoped not to hit a creaking floorboard, but the chambers were so well cared for the floors remained silent. With my hand upon the handle, I slowly turned it, no lock or key to the door it slowly opened. An empty room, a large pillar, held the roof to the centre. Nothing but a beam of the hidden moon passed through the windows, but as I turned to leave, I saw it, or him.

Shivering in a corner, he stood, no longer in tattered clothes, but still poorly fed, wearing a gown of white. Billy was unrecognisable.

"Billy?" I whispered, launching towards him. The fear in his eyes sent cold draught through me. His hands were shaking, holding a finger to his panicked lips.

"Don't wake the master, he doesn't enjoy being woken."

"Billy, what happened?" I quivered, looking at the rope that bound his wrists. I quickly shook to untie them. He pulled his arms away. "Billy, please, let me help you."

"I was a good boy, Rose."

"He is a good boy, Rose." Ben stood at the doorway. Falling to the floor, I looked at the horrifying shadow in the doorway.

"What did you do?" I scowled at him. Hate and fury clashed with bitter fear and rage.

"'Twas not what I did, Rose, you brought him here, what did you expect?" Billy's pitiful

eyes looked towards me, filled with the suffering
he had experienced, the pain the boy had felt, I
was a monster, the evils of the chambers had all
come from me.

"Ben, please," I crawled to his feet,
remaining, begging, "Let him go, you cannot do
this to a child."

"I will do what I need to in order to keep
the lions happy, as will Billy, won't you, Billy?"

I looked at the poor creature sat by the
wall. He nodded, squinting his eyes as he did.

"Up you get, Rose," Ben asked, but I
ignored, I felt him boil, reaching down he took a
clump of my hair, forcing a scream as I leapt to
my feet, dragging me from the room, down the
corridor and carelessly bumping me down each
step, death left a hard lump in my throat. He
dragged me across the balcony and back to my
quarters. I had known pain; the beatings of
children pale compared to a beating from a man.
I had upset Ben, and I was sorry, but he did not
listen to my words of begging, instead he bruised
my ribs with his fists, he avoided my face, instead
of swinging me by my hair from bed to chair,
throwing me through the room. The night was lit
with my screams, but no one came. My door
remained closed. His violation of every part of
me had my lesson learnt. I would never anger
him again.

He escaped Billy, using my beating to climb from the window and towards the streets below. I had saved one life, but I had caused great pain to many others. Something needed to change.

"Francis, so glad to see you," he stood in my doorway.

"I received a letter, delivered to me by Fredrick. I believe you need to speak with me?"

"I do, and I know you have little time, but please, the chambers have changed. They are taking children, Francis, innocent children." His face reddened, storming from the chambers I stood proud at my door as he bolted towards Benjamin looking smug at the bar, muffled words of anger from Francis met me, I saw Benjamin look towards me, his mouth drew down in horror, knowing I was the one, I had put right my wrong, and now Francis would ensure no others would suffer by his hand. Shoving him away from prying ears, Francis and Benjamin forced their way through the chambers.

The winters came and went further and further. Almost seven years had passed within the chambers, and I still had nothing for myself. My routine did not exist. I would wake, work, and sleep. The town was nothing but a crumbling ruin beneath me; I had no dealing with that place now; I had no desire, to run, to hide or to die, nothing was good anymore, the men coming to my chambers to share in my vice were the only faces I saw, those within the crowds of my stage were blank, no expressions, no feelings, nothing.

I had watched from closed doors as the world wasted. Mr McNeil, who owned land toward the north near Gallows Hill, he told me of a clause in his will, with no son or daughter, he gifted the land to the town, the moment Benjamin found out, they mysteriously caught Mr. McNeil in fraudulent dealing with the Earl of Thembrooke, whilst the Earl escaped relatively unscathed, Mr. McNeil was not so lucky, they wanted his land; they hanged him on the morn of his birthday.

'Twas a harsh place, I would take them to worlds of unimaginable pleasure, but they always wanted more, with a threat of my bottle running dry, I gave more, I had reached the winter of my years, I had entered the chambers as a lady, but I would leave as a squawking whore.

Francis barely visited me now. He knew what I was. They talked about it enough in the lower hall, drifting voices would always seep through the crack in my door. Awaiting my next victim of my forked tongue, I hoped to see Francis that day, but he came and left without so much as a glance toward my balcony.

Claudia would often pay me a visit, trying to force me to eat something. The bitter taste of food had become painful to me, even water was ash in my mouth.

"Eat something, Rose, you'll waste away. There was never much on you to begin with."

"I don't want food." I looked from the window. The streets below were silent. Darkness had taken them long ago.

"Rose, please," I could hear her begging, but nothing made sense to me anymore. "You must understand, I know this place is a hard place to be at times, but you know too much. There is nowhere they can send you now, apart from one." A sorrow in her eyes met the tears in mine. "Rose, if you cannot cope here, they will send you to the Lions boneyard."

"The Gallows." I knew exactly what she was talking about.

"Benjamin isn't happy with you, or me. We need to survive, Rose, no matter what."

"Pass me my bottle, please?" I had the urge, but I knew it was that which was keeping me here, a prisoner with no chains.

"No," she quickly stood. I did not understand her frustration. "Rose, you need to listen, look in the mirror and see what that stuff has done to you, please, Rose." Her begging fell upon deaf ears, I was not willing to listen, through everything, my rape, mental anguish, through the pain of betrayal, the only thing that had been there for me, the only thing to see me through, was my tincture, 'twas my saviour, and I would not abandon it, like so many had abandoned me.

She left, saying few more words, which always felt like a dull sound of the wind. I did not listen anymore; she had taken me into the chambers for her own gain. Benjamin had joined the chambers, offering a life of misery and torment. I did not know who I was, my purpose, my fate. Moving about my room, I sat at my dressing table. I would sit there each day, painting my face to hide the sores, to hide the tired eyes, the sagging of my skin and horrid grey complexion. The more I stared, the more I realise my friend, the only thing to have seen me through the hardest of times, 'twas killing me, and I needed to end it, before it ended me.

I cried, hard. I spent the entire night reaching for that bottle but refusing to let my hand tighten, refusing to pick it up. Such difficulties was something I was not used to. I had risen from adversity; I had seen the best of days in the workhouse, watching the flowers sway in the breeze in the meadow, and I had felt the worst, having sore fingers and hands from sewing cotton garments and threading the tiny needles, my hands had bled, I had slept without food or water, but little Rose, she could always find the bright side of life, I could always find the sun in the mist, the flower among bramble, I could no longer see that, my tincture had forced me into a life of sin, but I would be the only one to break free from that. I had never tried before, ending my need for my tincture was far too daunting. I had felt the chest pains, the stomach pains without it, but I had never pushed through, I had never broken from it; I had always given in to it, allowing it to take me on a journey, free from worry and pain, free from my future.

The mirror was cruel, calculating; I was still young, but within its silver abyss an elderly woman, alone, sad, and old glared back at me, I did not want to die alone, but I was forcing it, madness filled my veins, not knowing who to trust, what to trust or how to fix the abomination of my life. I was mistaken to think I could ever be a lady; I was nothing but a child of misfortune, dredged from the deepest depths of the Trent, forced to work as a child because my parents could not hold on to life, I would be nothing, forever left to wander the streets, searching for the next man to take me, just hoping to find shelter. A heavy rain outside freshened the air, I used to love the smell of fresh fallen rain, but it brought vomit to my lungs, thrashing on the bed the pain in my gut churned, a burrowing animal inside me begged to escape the pits of darkness.

"Rose!" I heard the scream. "Rose!" a man screamed, too. My eyes were not my own. Seeing clouds of darkness cover the room, I hit the lowest point of my life.

"Water!" he yelled; the voices were there but faces were none. "Get her some water!"

"Is she going to die?" a second man asked.

"No," he snapped, "Back to your room... Claudia, water now!" his yelling roused me, fluttering my eyes I saw the blurred face of Ben. "What did you do?" he snarled at me, angry with my attempt to let my vice go. "Rose, what did you take?"

His screaming only made me wince. "It isn't what she took, it's what she didn't." Claudia stood behind him, holding a small cup of water. Crouching down towards me, she calmed her voice. "Rose, you tried to stop, didn't you?"

"Stop what?" Benjamin had no clue of the pain I was in; I could still feel the burning deep within.

"Her vice, Ben." Her eyes did not leave mine, she could see my pain, because she had felt it herself, so many years ago, I felt it in her, I could see the memories flood her mind of the horror she had seen the day she gave up her vice. "Rose, you can't just stop, it would kill you."

"I don't want this," I cried, so hard I cried a desperation to escape from that place. That world had gripped me. "I can't do this, Claudia."

She turned to Ben. "I'm sure you liked her, once." He looked terribly confused. "Your talks each morning and at night, well, your pushing, your insisting she finds out more, your abuse of children! This is what it does, what you did to her." her jaw clenched, looking at him in disgust. "She invites death, Ben, because that is what this place is..."

"What are you talking about?" he asked as he stood, slowly rising from the bed as though poised for a battle of wits.

"Don't be so stupid, that's why the boy was here, Rose told you, many times she said the men in this place want younger, they want their demons to be tamed by allowing them the filth of flesh, allowing them to explore their most forbidden selves..."

"The boy is no more!" Ben shouted, enraged.

"He is now, from hell to a place worse than this," Claudia stepped towards him.

"There is no place worse than this..." my muttering madness made sense to them, they looked towards me.

"There is, Rose," Claudia leant towards me, a madness in her eyes was something I had never seen before. She hated me. "You insisted they listen to what the animals want, and you brought a child into the lion's lair, to be brutalised by these monsters." I felt her brewing. She had been my friend, my confidant, my passion for staying. She stepped back. The window was ajar.

"You are just animals. I could take it, what they did to me, what they forced me to endure with a smile I took it for so long! But a child! Who knows nothing of this world or the monsters in it!"

"We did him a favour. He would've starved otherwise!" Benjamin's argument was weak.

"A favour. If you think that a favour, then you are worse than those who see his demons each night, those who took him and forced his suffering..."

"I fed him, clothed him!" his screaming forced her back towards the window. We were not normal people. The chambers had changed us, mutilated our very souls, and weakened our spirits to nothing.

"You have no power here, Benjamin," she muttered. "They took everything from me. I could cope with your beatings, but this, to see an innocent child suffer like this, Benjamin! To see what you have done! I can see this no more!" I remained silent on the bed. Tears filled her eyes, forcing their way into her mouth. The bitterness she felt that day was something I never wanted for myself. "I'm sorry, Rose. This was my fault. I never should've let John go." Her eyes were red with tears, her reddened face looked to Benjamin, who remained weakened and still beside me. "You will suffer for this. You killed him for a secret he knew nothing about. Let us die in peace..."

"He's dead?" I heard myself whimper. I believed I had saved him, but I had caused his suffering before his death. A thud met us as her body hit the ground below. I heard a shudder, 'twas myself clambering toward the window, desperately screaming 'No!' it did nothing. Claudia left me.

The days were colder, the nights were darker. I returned to the one friend I had, my chainless prison, my tincture. Exploring the world of freedom was a dream to me once, but with my tincture, my vice, 'twas a reality, I could see it, feel it, explore it, and always in the company of an animal, the lions of the chambers were true beasts, they demanded more from me, each night I would double my usual clients, although Benjamin had kept his secret within the chambers, I was the only woman there, just as Claudia once was, not a part of my body left untouched by a man's hand, I was weakened by my tincture, and they were weakened by me, strength was slowly returning to me, my nights busied with visiting men, gave me more freedom from my vice.

The death of Claudia, as sad as it was, came as a saviour to me. The day of the funeral was a meagre turnout, the mourners were few, me and the priest of the church buried her in

Broad Marshes, no one remembered her that day, the men she had pleased over the years proved she was nothing to them, nothing but flesh.

Claudia had changed my life, not for the worst. I had entered the chambers with my free will. Leaving them was no option now, but I could, at least, make the most of my stay there while it lasted. My pact to Claudia, upon the day of her funeral, was to prove her wrong, I would find strength to abandon the chambers, I would walk free from those walls and live a fulfilled life of peace, how I would do this, I was yet to figure out, but seeing her fall from that window, reserved that her only escape was death, it convinced me, I would not become Claudia, I would break free from the Lions Chambers, one day.

A knock at my door roused me, I was expecting no more guests that evening, but the solemn face of Francis looked to me from the shadows of the corridor, removing his hat to his chest as he walked inside, it shocked me to see him.

"What a surprise, a pleasant surprise. I try to avoid such situations now."

"I apologise for my absence, Rose, it's only," he was awkward. He knew what I had become and felt embarrassed to be there with me. "Well, you know what it is, Rose."

"I'm a whore, Francis, you can say it..."

"No, I can't, because that was never my intention. I saw you as company and they have used you for so much worse..."

"For the sake of my life, you know that, Francis, but you did not deliver me here, neither did Gladys nor Tom. I did that myself. This is my mistake, now I must come to terms with that."

His smile was fleeting as he sat. They wore his usual chair from the many visitors it had received. "I admire your strength. What is happening in that head of yours brings me a different fear."

"My head is as clear as the day I arrived here, only stronger. What brings you here, Francis?"

"Thoughts," he replied with raised brows. His attire had not changed. He did not follow the fashion as many others did. "If only she knew." He placed his hands on his head as he hunched over. "She would hate me for this."

"Who?" I quickened towards him. I cared for Francis. He was not like the others.

Lifting his head, his face filled with tears. "Your mother."

From that moment, I knew what death felt like. "Who are you, Francis, to me?"

"Your uncle," his shame was clear upon his face. "I married your mother's sister, but they fell out, over the state of your father." His dark words shuddered me to the core. "He was a drunkard, a man of no reputation, and when your parents died, we didn't have the capabilities to raise a child by then. Besides, it would've caused issues within local government..."

"Government?" I could hardly breathe as I stood to confront him. "What has government to do with the life of a child, with family?"

"Everything, Rose, if I took you in, then I would sacrifice everything I had, and I had little as it was..."

"Little, a mansion on the outskirts of town, a salary to feed the thousands. How is that little? How selfish can one be?"

My screeching voice shocked him to stand. "Rose, I could not take in a child of such a poor reputation. This is not my burden 'twas your parents..."

"Burden? I was a child, Francis, not capable of such things. I was not a drunkard, I was not them, they were still hard-working people..."

"Is that what they told you?"

"'Tis what I remember."

"Then you remember wrong." He came closer to me. Secrets and lies seemed to have become the foundation of my life. How far their deceit went, I was yet to discover. "What you remember is a fairy-tale, a fantasy, that is all. What you remember is false. It sometimes happens to victims of abuse. You, Rose, were doomed from the moment you were born."

"What are you talking about?" My confusion only deepened as Francis calmed. "Francis, what are you talking about?"

"Sit, child, and I will explain. I have made peace with my demons, and now I must make peace with yours." I slowly sat, waiting for his poor excuse. "This town, this place, it is tainted, but we do it for a reason, we rid this town of the detritus of the streets, those too lazy to feed themselves, those too incapable, those who have little care or feeling towards others, we build this town brick by brick, and a single mistake can bring it down to ashes. I could not take you in, but I could have you sent to the workhouses, a place of safety."

"Hundreds die in workhouses, but you were willing to take that chance with your own family?"

"I married into it, you are not my blood, Rose, I did what I had to as a favour, and the day I saw you in the town I saw your mother looking back at me, I brought you here to keep an eye on you, it wasn't until I realised how bad your addiction was that I regretted my decision, and now the room of Claudia is empty, yours forever full, I do not believe you have long left here..."

"Claudia once told me you were the one to rid the chambers of their burdens."

"It's a disgusting truth, but not all true. Rose, I had only one family member, my wife, and now with her gone I have only you, although no one else knows this..."

"Well, they do now," Benjamin, he wormed his way into the conversation through a gap in the door. "This is all fascinating, Francis, please, go on."

Francis seemed to age a decade. His hands shook as Benjamin towered over him, waiting for him to speak. "Family means someone to threaten. I did as they commanded for fear they would harm my wife and I would lose my reputation."

"True, and this explains why you have been rather lazy of late, Francis. I asked you to pass the death sentence to 3 people this month. Now I know why you failed to do so."

"There was hope for those men. They were no threat to you or this town..."

"They were a threat to our economy, our everything."

"They were a threat to no one!" I hardly saw Francis's temper fray. My concern grew.

"Well, at least now we know, not only do you hold stakes in this business, you hold more here than most."

Francis's blue fearful eyes looked at me, a piercing look of fear I had never seen radiated from those eyes. His terror hit me.

Benjamin disappeared as quickly as he had arrived. "Francis, what does this mean?"

"It means they have their weapon back. If I do not do as they please, they will hurt, injure and even kill you." He seemed to hold no feelings, no fear of reprisal. "I failed you once, Rose. I will not fail you again."

"Then we leave, I leave this place, I leave the country, I need to be free, Francis, please..."

"You can't, Rose, it takes money to leave..."

"You have plenty..."

"In property, I invest, it is what built my home, it is what keeps this town growing, investing in building, people, and places, I have enough to feed myself of a month, Rose, not enough to free you from these bonds, but we will find a way."

"When?" My desperation grew, a lifetime of torment had caught me in that moment, the workhouse was nothing but legal torture for children, the chambers were torture for women, I had never escaped my past, but now Francis could help me.

CHAPTER TWELVE NEVER AFTER

Months passed in the chambers, Francis was the last to forsake me, I was through with lies and deceit, there was no one there for me now, no one who would help me, no one to free me from my invisible bonds, I had become the very thing I hated; I was no lady; I was nothing but a whore.

I filled my days avoiding that bottle, the very thing that had forced me here. I needed a clear head, and I would only take it when they took it with me. Every evening they felt a delightful bliss, I secretly enjoyed the passion in my wake of merriment and delight, I took them to places they never knew existed, Claudia did not have her addiction to lessen her guilt, but I did, and it helped.

Francis was absent for months, seeing him below the balcony caused me some distress at first, but a new friend was by his side, a large man, a man I remember from the streets of Nottingham, I would often see him upon the steps of the Gaol, tipping his hat toward me believing me to be a lady, those days were as dead as my soul.

Each night I would glance towards him, hoping he had a plan for escape, but nothing. Weeks and months came and went. My happy ever after was fading into the dark bricks of the chambers, into my own never after.

"Will you dine with me this evening?" Benjamin stood at my door. Each time I saw his face, I refused to look him in his viper eyes, for fear of falling into the hell he had made for me.

"Do I have a choice?" I sat silently by the window. The smell of a fresh spring rain filled the room, the only freshness I had smelt in a while.

"Not really, I'm your manager, and you are here to please me."

"In more ways than one, I assume?" I could not change my snapping tone towards him. I hated him now. My dark shadow was nothing but a demon.

"Rose, you must get over this. I've noticed you're not taking your tincture as much. Your vice is not what keeps you here..."

"Oh, and there was me thinking it was something far more disturbing. I know what this is." I stood, for once I would face the creature. "John, Francis, Claudia, even you, you're all just as animalistic, I simply do what I do in order to survive, nothing more and nothing less, I have no thanks to give you or the chambers."

"Your loyalty flails."

"My loyalty has always been with one, and only one, I simply got lost along the way."

"Do you even know what the chambers have given you? Do you even appreciate the magnitude of these chambers?"

"I appreciate only one, myself. I've survived so far, and if you think I will remain here forever, you're very mistaken..."

"They will chew you up and spit you out, little girl, the chambers are your only home, this is the only place you would ever be welcome, the chambers are not bricks and mortar, they are breathing people, powerful people who will not allow your poison tongue to sully their reputation, be careful what you wish for, Rose, dreams are not far from nightmares."

The room warmed as soon as he left. He brought an icy chill to my blood. The silent night gave me much to ponder, but I still had a plan in mind. I would escape that place fairly and without reprisal.

Come the morning, the chambers were empty. I would usually plan on visiting the town on Wednesdays, but today seemed far too dull outside. Choosing one of my finest dresses, a gift from Baron Von Haart, I made my way to the balcony, whereupon seeing Benjamin, I felt my blood cool again.

"Off out?"

"Of course, I have my routine, Ben. I would thank you to allow me to keep that part of my freedom at least."

He bowed his head. "You're many things, Rose, but you're not stupid. I'll see you back here before the doors open."

I took a chance that day. Perhaps it was a step too far, but I turned to my right. Benjamin stood in horror as he watched me leave through the front door. I was through using the back door like a simple slave, my sacrifice had saved the chambers, I knew Benjamin would not stop me, I walked proud from the doors that day, receiving several hat tips from some of the real gentlemen, those who did not indulge in activities of the chambers.

The market that day was busy, new materials were being brought in ready for the festive Easter period, the ladies of the town wore bright colours during Easter, for me, 'twas an excuse to spend my wage on something other than tincture and jewellery. Passing through the market, the sheriff's men followed my path. I knew them all. They were not there to hinder me, they were there to protect me.

The Weekday Cross offered shelter from the gathering crowds. But that smell hindered me, the smell of the fish market. It reminded me of them, Gladys, and Tom. I trusted the devils with my life, and they delivered me into hell.

"Rose, you don't have to," Connor was a sweet man, a stranger to the truth of the town, he knew the chambers were not a place for weak men, but he failed to see past the lime plaster to the truth in the walls.

"Gladys and Tom are not my concern anymore, Connor. Thank you for your concern though."

"Always, Rose." I know he had some unearthly feeling for me. He would often glance towards my room when in the chambers, but he would never visit me in my quarters. He seemed like a proper gentleman, not the type to indulge in such sordid activities.

I saw her, shamelessly selling her wares in the window of the new shop they had built, they had made a business from me, I was more than an investment to them, I was their business, the fish they sold was nothing but a front for their sordid dealing with the sales of people.

I had the courage to go near the shop. Looking through the window, I saw her face, sagged and old. Age had not been kind to her, and I was glad. I had never felt true hate before. Now I knew what it felt like to truly hate someone.

The chambers offered no comfort that evening; I had no plan to escape. My faith in Francis had failed me, and then he came.

Toward the end of the evening, a quiet knock at the door sounded sweet, innocent. I would usually wait for my assistant to invite people in, but they had called him away on other business. My schedule was empty. I was expecting no one.

"Who is it?" I called out, hoping it was not Benjamin come to mock me again.

"Ma'am, the name's Joe," his voice shuddered, his nerves were clear within his tone. "I've come for a talk is all."

It was an odd request now; a few years had passed since conversation was at the top of a gentleman callers list. Upon opening the door, a dishevelled brown-haired man stood, green eyes glared towards me, his slim face gave a sign of youthfulness I did not expect.

"Please," I invited him in, "are you new to the chambers?"

"Very, ma'am," he replied, holding a hat between his hands. He did not dress like the others, his style clearly held some influence. "My brother-in-law, he insists the chambers would be good for me." His piercing eyes looked at me. "Now I understand they probably will."

"You know who I am?" I held doubt with the words he spoke. I did not believe he knew my duty there.

"Of course, ma'am, you're a lady, and it would honour me to join you this evening," his quivering voice warmed me.

I had heard no one call me a lady in that way before. He besotted me. Reaching out, I held his shaking hands.

"And it would honour me for you to join me. I have not eaten yet. I could have something brought in?"

His eyes warmed me as he looked from the floor, piercing my soul to the core, "I would enjoy that, very much."

As we seated at the table, I awaited our meal for the evening, 'twas a glad change to my usual routine. "How long have you been in Nottingham?"

"Not long. I left the ship nearly a month past."

"Your ship? Do tell?"

"It wasn't all that interesting, the war in the Americas had me held for over two years, I returned here upon hearing of my mother's passing, my father and I, we don't get along so well, but my brother-in-law is welcoming, as is my sister, Isabelle, Francis and George seem close and I simply came here upon George's request."

"He sounds like he cares for you. The Lions Chambers are a place where men become gentlemen, 'tis a place of invested business. You will do well here."

"I already have, Ma'am..."

"Please, call me Rose, everyone else does."

"I know... Rose," he seemed nervous, but his smile grew. He sat forward from his chair and took my hand in his, his hands were cold and rough. He had lived a life of freedom upon the waves. "Tis why I came here, to meet the Rose of Nottingham. So many speak of you, your intriguing voice which lights the bleak Nottingham nights, your ability to see light in darkness." I felt my smile wither as he spoke. "You are a gem of this town, Rose, they all speak of you."

"Me?" It confused me. I knew nothing of this.

He slowly nodded his head, a look of wonder in his eyes spoke of the intrigue in his heart. "You are famed throughout Nottingham, to Lincoln and beyond. I first heard your name on the shores of America. You have supporters, Rose."

"Supporters," my confusion worsened. I never thought I was so well known, but known for what was a thought that sickened me. "What part of my duty do they support?"

He took a moment, sitting back in his chair, he thought. I know he did not wish to offend me, but I strived for honesty. "The earl of Norrington, he tells of a woman who has taken the chambers from a wreckage to a place of true conversing, a place where all gentlemen are welcome, a place where you find yourself lulled into deep relaxation by a lady who sings sweeter than a songbird, you see the Lions Chambers are in many counties, they have one in Lincoln, London, Devon, even Portsmouth have chambers, they never invited me into them, but men talk, and most talk is of a delicate flower of Nottingham, one that every chambers strives to own..."

"Own! I am no object to be swapped and owned..."

"I didn't mean to offend," he panicked, seeing my disgust in his words. "Please, I simply mean, it is an honour to meet someone of such notoriety, someone who has warmed the hearts of so many."

"I find it rather unnerving I knew nothing of this. I did not know my name has spread so."

"Many of the men here travel on business, most of the chamber's house them while they work in their areas, this is how news spreads of your dedication, they speak of returning to Nottingham, to see their Rose, but so many speak of it, I simply wished to come here and see you myself."

"So, the only reason you came to Nottingham, was to meet me?"

He nodded. His smile warmed the room. Such hope was in his eyes, such expectation for a woman who was nothing but the whore of the chambers.

"I am saddened to disappoint, but I am not the Rose they speak of." His smile withered, like a wilting flower, his eyes drooped. "I may have been, once, but such hope of becoming the lady I once so wished to be, it has gone, drained from me, I was on the right path once, Joe, then I came here, to Nottingham, every hope, every dream, it bled from me, I will never be the Rose of Nottingham they spoke of, I am sorry, Joe, but I have wasted your journey."

"No," he whispered as he stood. He could see something in me, something which had died long ago. "She is still in there, Rose, my journey to the other world has been arduous, dangerous, and frightening, but the only thing that kept me going, the only thing that made me want to return, was meeting you, the Rose they all spoke of so lovingly, I always wanted to be a part of that, they never spoke of their wives, their family, always Rose, you, I returned alive, because of you."

He seemed insane. I never thought I had brought such fame to myself; I was nothing in the chambers, but upon the streets, in mouths of gentlemen, I was the Rose of Nottingham.

"Your voice, Rose, I want to hear it. I have dreamed of the day I could visit these chambers to hear you sing."

"Well, I will be here tomorrow. I look forward to seeing you then. For now, I must remain humble. I did not know any of this, Joe, and I struggle to trust..."

"You can trust me, Rose, please." His desperate plea spoke truth, quivering lips, and eyes. He could barely spring together a sentence.

"So, you are now a member here?"

"I am. George and my father paid for my entrance into the chambers. Although they do not need me there, I am here to simply show face. I would rather show it here, with you."

He was in love with me, a woman who he had met barely a moment ago, he had spent years pondering over me, it flattered me, but my past kept me humble, Joe was a kind soul, not the type who would usually pass through, I did not want him to become tainted by the chambers as so many had before.

"I am duty-bound here, Joe. I must warn you, whatever you think of me, 'tis not the full truth."

"I know what they do to you, what they allow them to do, Rose, but I'm not here for that. I will not judge you," he rushed towards me. I jumped back, still fearful of men. "I will break you from these bonds, Rose, I will free you."

I had never had such a rush of emotion before, so many others were far too concerned for their own reputation, they would never help me, but Joe would, he cared not for matters of business, he cared for matters of the heart, just like me. He was a true gentleman, and with him by my side, I would again become a lady.

The town that morning seemed brighter, the loud building works along Clumber Street and even within the alley of Greyhound Street seemed to dull. The sound of birds could finally reach my ears. A scent of wildflowers freshly picked reached me from the bottom of Chapel Bar, where a young girl and her mother would set up a stall to sell their field flowers. I had no choice but to buy some. Such beauty did not belong on the streets.

The days were brighter; I had a plan to escape slowly developing; I knew I could not do it alone, and now I knew they all knew me. Every large town knew the Rose of Nottingham, but Joseph would be my escape.

CHAPTER THIRTEEN A GENTLEMAN'S FRIEND

That night I sang, as strong as I could to impress Joseph who remained at the bar, with my performance finished, I made my way toward my quarters awaiting his visit, he would not let me down, I could feel it in my blood, his rushing desperation hit me with every note I sang, every word shattered his heart with a thousand daggers, he was mine to do with as I wished.

"Your reputation proceeds you." His smile grew further. From ear to ear, I had pleased him. "I was speechless at the bar, Rose."

"I assume you booked your place here this evening?"

"I did, in fact, Francis went to the trouble of booking the entire evening with you, he said it took a lot, you have many wishing to see you, and now I know why, I never thought I would hear the angels sing in this life, but here you are."

"I can hardly compare myself to angels..."

"I can. I have seen the hardest of days, but your voice makes everything worth it. I know my struggle was worth everything now."

"You flatter me, please, carry on," I joked. He chuckled as he sat.

"I could sit here all night passing compliments to you, and I would be glad to do so, but I feel something more important is in line for this evening."

I took a breath, knowing what I wanted to ask, but scared to ask the question. "Tell me about your family, your brother-in-law, and sister. They sound lovely."

He took a sip of tea I'd had brought in; I took him as the kind of gentleman who cared more for a feminine touch than most. Tea was a fine choice for Joseph. "My sister Isabelle, she's sweet, sometimes too sweet, she sees the world for the good it does, not for the cruelty that often comes from that good, George is a different creature, well put together, but I fear his eyes are closed to the world, the real world, their children are delightful, but once again, what do children know of reality."

"More than you realise, we were all children once, and we all grew, knowing the world is often cruel and unfair."

"True, my father is a quiet soul, I wronged him, many years ago, it forced me into the Kings Navy, I was grateful for that, but I would have preferred staying at home, when in battle, being frightened is difficult to hide, but fear is something that must remain hidden..." he took a pause, looking towards me in my comfort, I felt light with Joe, I did not feel rushed, the night was ours, and I intended to keep it that way.

"Are we in favour with the war?"

"Who knows, I hardly left the shore. I fought once, and that was enough, seeing that was enough to keep me a peaceful man for the rest of my days. Tell me about your parents?"

"I would rather not speak of it." I was awkward about them now. I trusted Joe, but I did not trust my past. I was not at fault for anything that happened, but I was at fault for believing such lies. "My parents have recently shown to have a shady past at best, and I do not indulge in such things. They frown upon speaking ill of the dead."

"Parents, they're savage at times, but usually with reasons, they all have their own demons, as we all do."

I leant forward. I wanted to show a flirtatious side towards Joe. I had his heart, but his mind was something I was yet to catch. "Tell me of your demons, Joe."

"Most of them are still in the docks at Portsmouth," he chalked, "my demons are far away yet, but I fear they will find me one day, I only hope that on the day they do, they find me in the arms of a beautiful woman."

I shuddered at the thought. I could have settled once, a husband, a family, but now I was far too tainted. I would bring dishonour to any husband.

"I am not that woman, Joe. I regret to be the one to let you down, but I have far more demons than you'll ever have, and I do not wish to share them."

"You will, eventually, I understand trust, it's hard to gain, but I will get it, Rose, I do not wish to make you uncomfortable, but you deserve better than this place, at the moment I can't give you that, but I will."

"I don't know why you would wish to do any of this for me. I'm nobody, Joe."

"No, you're the lady who made sure I came home, the way they spoke of you, like a fallen angel, here for their pleasure." His tone twisted to a tone of hate. "They used you, Rose. They speak of you with such love and caring, but the reality is, they use you."

"'Tis what I'm here for, all I know, all I'll ever be..."

"No, Rose, you can run, we can run."

"You said it yourself. The chambers stretch further than we could ever run. They will find me, and they will not allow me to return here. I know their secrets."

"Then you can use that against them, either they let you go, or you tell the world."

"I've had this conversation before. Who will believe the word of a whore over the word of esteemed gentlemen? Not only a common whore but one with a deadly vice for that matter."

"Vice?"

"Opium, Joe, that bottle contains the chains which keep me bound to these chambers. I sing, and I do what I do to remain sane."

"Have you tried to stop?" 'twas a stupid question, however, he did not know the grip of laudanum, he had never felt the overwhelming need, the pain without it was unbearable.

"I cannot, Joe, I have tried. It almost killed me, and it killed Claudia, but I have decreased my need for it. That, I fear, is as far as it will go." I leant forward. He was such a sweet man, gentle, honest, and kind, a king of gentlemen. I could never allow him to risk anything for my sake. "Do not try to tame me, Joe, you will fail, do not try to take me from these chambers, they will hunt us down and end us both, please, just take this time as a pleasure we can see each other, nothing more."

His disappointment was shattering, I hardly knew this man, and he hardly knew me, but something deep down spoke of an earthly bond we shared, he had found himself captive in his career, forced to fight a war he had no hand in, his loyalty forcefully placed at someone else's feet, just as I had. The chambers were my hold; they were a place of safety once, but now they were a place of painful pleasure, the men were no good, they would struggle to please a wife and I would not be the one to teach them, I had a role to play, a cheap actress forced to take to the stage of an unjustifiable patriarchy, they were not gentlemen, Joseph was my gentleman, and he gave something I had not felt in a long time.

Standing at my window I watched the crowds pass outside, their business was normal, their worries of money were nothing compared to the worries of body and mind, the worries of the eternal soul, my soul felt tainted, but I knew Joseph could help me get it back.

I thought that day, long and hard, I knew I had to leave. The lions of the chambers were willing to do anything to keep their darkness in the shadows. William, the poor boy, I missed him so, each time I thought of him I remembered his face, looking at me from the bins below my window.

The evening lingered, not a single sign of Joseph met me that evening, I had known him for a few days, but I missed him, my usual brutal callers came and went, they had their way with the Rose, not knowing the thorns she held.

Joseph did not show that evening, but another caller, one I did not expect, knocked at my door. He slowly entered, a fresh glow had appeared on his face. I felt glad knowing Francis was well. Even though he had remained distant from me, I did not wish to keep such ill feelings towards him.

"Good evening, uncle," I nodded. The sarcasm was something he could do without, but it was my way of showing my anger towards him.

"Good evening, Rose, may I?" he pointed his palm to the chair.

"Always, you needn't ask." My bitterness broke with his solemn tone. "You've been busy of late?" I drew the curtains, not wanting to allow the outside world into our private conversation. "I noticed that you've been in the chambers less and less, I must say, simply hearing your voice down there brings great comfort to me."

"It is good to know, but I struggle within these walls, Rose. You must know why."

I shook my head, unaware of the care he held for me. "I cannot even fathom a guess."

"Well, it is hard, Rose, knowing what is happening up here, while, down there, I have to speak to these men, knowing the beasts they are, they did not mean the chambers to be used for this, and after what happened to William..."

I looked at him over my shoulder, "Please, do not speak of it."

Unable to still his lips he slowly spoke, "He was a lost cause, Rose, after what happened here, after what they did to him, we rid those men from the chambers, we should not allow such creatures in places such as this."

"What happened to Benjamin? He's still here."

"He is here for a reason, Rose. He will get his, but I fear the walls may have ears. We must speak carefully."

"Speak all you must. Billy suffered, as no child should ever suffer, and what then? Put to the streets as a stray dog, hunted like an animal."

"Rose, what happened with Billy happened for a reason. Billy would never have been the same again, Rose. We did him a favour, no struggle, no worry, most importantly, no pain..."

"No tongue, you mean, no way of telling the outside world what happens here?"

"I hate who the chambers have turned me into, Rose, but I do this for you, for my family." I could see his eyes flicker, struggling to hold the lies. A hard stare toward him loosened his tongue. "I tried, alright, I tried to argue the point that the boy was innocent, both of them, but the board insisted that nothing good could ever come of this. The only way to ensure that was to ensure he never spoke again. It doomed even the boy he befriended from the moment he met him."

"You are a magistrate, Francis, you killed them both, their blood is on your hands..."

"Actually, that would be George..."

"Yours, Francis!"

"Poppycock, child you do not know the difficulties I face, if I did not do as they commanded I would lose everything, my house, the chambers, my title, but more importantly, you, I would lose you, Rose, I have only just gained you back in my life and not a single life will ever be as important to me as yours, now, are you going to invite me into pleasant conversation or continue to shout and point fingers of blame?"

His snapping forced me still. I lowered my tone. "Why did you come here, Francis... uncle?" I still loved him as I would any family. He was my uncle, his struggles were my own.

"I came here to ask a favour of you." I shook my head, wondering why I should do anything to help him. "We have a problem in the town, bodies are going missing from some graves, it isn't something we are too concerned about at the moment, but I know your room has a view toward the old brewhouse, where they now make medicines, I strongly suspect that these men of science have taken on an animalistic urge to experiment, all I ask is if you see anything odd you are to tell myself or one of the sheriffs men, they are aware of your position here, so please, all I ask is that you watch."

"Who else knows about this?"

"No one, we are keeping it strictly quiet for now, hoping family members of the deceased do not know. Just keep this to yourself, Rose."

"Of course I will, but I doubt I will see anything, the streets near the old brewhouse are far too dark, even the lamps below the window often struggle on cold and windy nights, we are slowly coming toward the autumn, I will try, but I can make no promises."

"And that Joe, chap," his mentioning of the name sent cold shivers through me. "Keep an eye on him. He is from a very trusted family, but I fear he may have another agenda. Keep your wits about you, Rose."

"I always do. Now, I can set such business aside. Tell me how you've been?" my sudden change of tone relaxed him.

"I would but I hardly have time, I'm sorry my darling, maybe next time." I cannot deny it disappointed me as Francis left, but I watched the window as he had asked me. Nothing happened that night or in the nights to follow. The streets were deader than the empty graves.

Family was a strange thought for me, but what I found odd was a father could see a son only once a month, but upon their reunion they would embrace and speak as though they had never been apart, I had lived a lonely life so far, being away from Joe, a man I hardly knew, hurt, 'twas a pleasurable pain, I must have liked him, I must have held feelings for him, otherwise I would not feel such pain. There was my pleasure, a pleasure in knowing I cared about someone. I did not believe Joseph would ever hurt me. I wished for my happy ending, but so much darkness upon those streets and within my quarters made it impossible to see such things. I was still a lost child, hoping for guidance.

I had saved myself more than once, with each man that came those following nights, as did a new mark or bruise. Now I knew why Claudia had the white powders in her room, to hide the bruises caused by brutal men. They ravaged me. They cared not for gentleness, animalistic and cruel were all they were.

Our nights in the chambers blossomed a friendship which I felt was different, Joe was not like the other men, he was a gentleman, a man who I could trust, I had struggled to trust since Gladys and Tom, in fact, they had haunted my thoughts, my nightmares filled with them. I was glad to have met Joe. Fate was at play each night he came to my quarters, but I was growing into something I never thought I was capable of. The prison in which I sat was keeping me from him, keeping me from a man who cared so deeply for me. He was willing to do anything to save me from this place. I would never have been here were it not for them. I forgave them once, but now I had Joe it trapped me. I no longer wanted to forgive them. I wanted to blame them; I wanted them to suffer as I had suffered.

So many years passed through my thoughts, I had taken to having a few drops of tincture each night before bed, but it no longer worked, watching a child being torn away from her parents who were incapable of caring for her, I was the child of my dreams, taken to a place which should've meant hope, but instead, 'twas a place of hate and greed, and then there was them, Gladys and Tom, who insisted on making my life more bitter for their own gain, they had done this, they were to blame, I could've had Joe, but what they had done to me kept us both apart.

CHAPTER FOURTEEN COMING AND GOING

Day after miserable day, I watched the dingy streets. Nothing. His body snatchers did not exist. I had convinced myself of this long ago, but Francis was a hard man to convince.

Joseph, my sweet Joseph, he would try to visit me, even sometimes during the day. The autumn struck hard that year. A chill hit the chambers that day. It would prove a fine day for venturing out. I looked forward to the market that day, stepping into the fresh morning, one of the sheriff's men stood upon the street, he would often stand outside the chambers ensuring the horse and carts remained slow through the town, so many accidents had taken innocent lives, especially in that area, where the fast roads met the slow roads, it would often lead to disaster.

My amble through the large market square filled with calling crowds and swollen streets, bodies packed tightly together. The busy day brought more surprise to me as I heard a calling in the crowd. Assuming 'twas one of the flower stalls selling their roses, I paid little attention to the name being called.

"Rose!" I heard a call through the swelling crowd, "Rose, please wait!" I turned frantically, realising the call aimed at me, I had seen them all upon the streets, those who would visit me within my chambers, but never would they acknowledge me, but the call was not from one of them, 'twas my Joseph, calling to me from the bustling crowds of frantic buyers.

"Joe!" I called out, hoping he would realise I was not ignoring him. Struggling through, I found a clearing. To the other side, there he stood, freely willing to notice me in public. By his side, a small woman stood wide with child. At first, my blood ran cold, thinking the worst, but she smiled at me.

Rushing to meet each other in the centre of the market square, she was the first to greet me. "You must be Rose. Joe talks of nothing else."

'Well, clearly she was no wife of his,' I thought, wondering who the enchanting woman was, her smile was bright and filled with the most spectacular glee I had ever seen, she seemed to carry happiness in her eyes, a light and hopeful heart showed in her rosy cheeks and locks of neat, curled hair.

"Ma'am," I curtsied to her. She was clearly older than me, she was clearly a lady of some standing. "My name is Rose, please. What has he been telling you?" I mockingly giggled.

"All good things. He tells me of your talents to sing the birds from the trees, he's been rather complimentary. I'm so sorry, where are my manners? I'm Isabelle, his sister."

"It is a pleasure to meet you. Joe was right. You certainly shine brighter than the sun." I remembered him speaking of her so warmly, her smile, her hair, even her brows. He spoke of her as he would a goddess of Greek.

"Well, it's good to know he has some kind words," she mocked.

We got on rather pleasantly; she was not like the other ladies of the town, those who would turn their head as soon as I got too close, they all knew what I was, Isabelle must have known, but she did not treat me like the others did, her smile was for me, her eyes met mine each time we spoke, she was such a beautiful spirit; she held no judgement towards me. I could've cried with joy at having met Isabelle. We spent the day shopping together, Joseph had told me plenty about Isabelle, that she married the town executioner, George, who I had often seen in the quiet corners of the chambers, but I did not judge him, the King's Court bestowed his duty.

Our morning ended far too quickly. "Please, can we meet again tomorrow? I've had such a lovely time, and although my duty begins soon, I have loved your company."

"Of course," her smile was luscious, she was such a beautiful spirit, I could not grasp how a woman like her could marry a man who made a living from death. "It would be my pleasure."

"Good, thank you, I look forward to seeing you later," I looked to Joseph, his welcoming arms had warmed me further, I never saw myself as part of a family, but Joseph had invited me in so freely, I knew he was a gentleman, but he shone above all others. "Will I be seeing you later?"

He looked to Isabelle, a sorry upon his brow worried me. "I will try to find time, but George has asked me to help with some business, but I will try my best."

"I know you will," my voice remained soft, I struggled to see what I could offer him, but I wanted to give him all I had, my heart, soul and mind, 'twas his now, he had shown a welcome I had never had, and for the first time since stepping into this cold and desolate world, I was happy, truly happy, not the false happiness of career or duty, but a comfortable happy, knowing I had someone in this miserable town who actually cared about me.

They passed by each night, coming and going from the sin they had left on me. I needed to escape. My hope was in the hands of a man who had forsaken me, 'twas what family was for, abandoning, but I had something else now, my Joe, I barely knew him, but he had shown me, willingly to his family, he had told me of the places he had seen, of the places he wished to take me. I was a woman, 'twas my duty in the chambers to enchant the men, but Joe had enchanted me, I wanted him, but not in the way they took me, I wanted his mind, his soul, his spirit, we would be together.

"I pay handsomely, you know that?" Joe sat upon my chair, waiting for me to sit, I seldom felt happy in the company of a man, but Joe was different, he was gentle, and he would never ask me for that.

"You pay what I am worth to you," I wobbled my head, hoping he would receive the joke.

"No, I haven't enough money in the world to pay what you're worth, but I am a man, Rose. I come to your quarters, most nights, but I leave here, intact."

His nervous laughter told me I had him caught. He was mine to do with as I wished. "You are different, Joe." I kept my voice low, my head bowed like a weeping bird. A weakness in my voice brought him closer to me. "I do like you, Joe, that is why I do not wish to sully what we have." My Rose-red lips pert towards him. I knew he wanted to kiss me. I felt my chest rise towards him. "I want you, Joe, but I want you differently. I want to give myself to you, as a proper lady, not a paid one." His eyes drifted to the floor; a disappointment struck him. "Joe, please, I do not wish to offend you, I wish to compliment you, what you did, in the town, no one has ever done that for me, it's usually turning heads of judgement, I am always met with such hate, but you changed that, you made me feel like a person, a real person, who really matters, I want nothing more than to have you in my bed, but I do not wish for payments, I wish to wait, and to see you in those sheets, when I am a lady again."

"You're my lady, Rose, always have been, and the first time I heard you sing, I knew then, you would be my everything, I know this is going to sound rather far-fetched..." I took my bottle from the table, ready for when he had finished, I felt the cramps in my arms, working towards my head. "I would love to be the gentleman you deserve, and I would spend every day of my life trying to be the man you need. I know I'm not much, Rose, but I'm nothing if not honest."

He was an honest man, my Joe. "It all seems like a dream, Joe, only thing is, I'm stuck here, until the day I turn grey and get thrown to the streets, there is no leaving the Lion's Chambers."

"Perhaps, but what if we had enough money to escape, to live forever in a small village, no towns, no cities, just us and the local cattle?"

"It's a wonderful dream, Joe, but that kind of money, it doesn't come from nowhere."

"No, but George is doing well..."

"You plan to rob him?" I mocked, "I've seen him, Joe, often with Francis but I see you nor Francis when he enters the bar, the man is enormous."

"But gentle, trust me, he has more heart than most." I could hear his sincerity. His silent plea was strange.

"The local executioner is a gentle soul. Does he use a silk rope on the necks of children?" my mocking clearly went too far, a scornful look met me. "Look, I don't doubt he is a good and kind man, but, Joe, helping a whore from her bonds in a gentleman's chambers, he is a patron here, 'twould be suicide if he so much as breathed a word of help."

"Maybe, but I'll figure something, I'm sure."

"Just stay safe, Joe, take care of yourself. 'tis the only way to ensure my happiness, your safety, you're all I really have."

"Don't say that, you're the Rose of Nottingham brightening these dismal streets with your voice. I didn't hear you tonight, though. I was busy."

"Doing what?" I slipped a small drop of tincture into my tea.

"Some project George has me on at work."

"You're working at the gaol?" I felt my heart sink. "Please, Joe, be careful there."

"Nothing to worry about, I just help with the... business he has there."

'Twas all very secretive, a side to him I had not yet seen. "So, this business, what does it entail?"

"Never mind, I would never put you at risk and this would..."

"Honesty, Joe, it is the foundation to any blossoming relationship." I didn't even realise I was doing it, the same tactics I would use to extract information from the lions I was using on Joe.

"Rose, please, it's dangerous..."

"Then I should know. I wish to know the duty my future husband involves himself in."

A look of glee brightened his eyes. A mystified look of love filled him. "Husband," I heard him whisper.

"If I can trust you, Joe, I cannot see why not."

He took a moment, his wandering eyes flickered through the room. I could see an internal battle within him.

"Rose," he whispered. He looked over my shoulder to the washroom behind. Taking my hand, he guided me there. "Just know this, George is a good man, too good in fact, he loses his life if they hear any of this." His whispers forced a quick nod from me, 'twas as good as a promise. I did not wish to feed Joe to the lions just yet. "All those nights I could not be here with you, was because I help George help them..."

"Them?"

"The innocent, so many are passing through the gaol, men starving, women forced to take to crime, even children, innocent children, he helps them escape, by making people think they're dead, he hangs them, but upon their burial, they take them from their boxes and set them free from Nottingham."

Such hope within his words had my heart pounding. Billy was all I could think of. This man may have saved him.

"Rose, you cannot breathe a word of this, just remember, if George can save them, it is possible he could save you."

My racing heart was hard to calm. I could only smile at his news. The hangman of Nottingham was not what people thought at all.

"Anyone who passes who is a true criminal, they leave them to god, but the others, they take them to Clifton. From there, they are free, forever."

Joe left my chambers warm with laughter and hope. I took no more tincture that evening, even with more coming and going. I kept my head clear, laid upon my pillow, and dreamed of the perfect place Joe had shown me. We shared dreams together, and so much more.

The streets were busy, no sheriff stood by the road that morning, carts came speeding through, ready to enter the bustling town. The market seemed in a silent mourning. Strangers seemed to mope in the streets, smiles were hard to find, not that they ever found me, anyway. A strange mood had come to the town, a mood I cared little for.

"Taking them? Where to, and what for?" I heard a passing conversation.

"Some awful things, things they call science, but we know it's sinister. Why else would they employ a snatcher of bodies?"

"I ope they catch em soon, got my aunt looking worse for wear at the moment, not long they said, and I can't afford all these medical people, nurses and the likes."

"Money snatchers," he proclaimed, "It's all they want from life, is money, 'swat science is, a way to take a life and make money from it."

The scepticism was shockingly eerie as the men passed by. Following the road to the market, a few ladies of the town walked toward me. Words similar to those men, words of bodies being taken from the Broad Marshes Burial ground took their usual glare over.

I tried to go about my day, but the air was thick with rumour. Talk of such dullness tainted my very complexion. I hurried back to the only place I knew to be more depressing. The chambers awaited me, my duty would soon begin, my hour upon an unwanted stage was upon me.

Dressed and ready I searched the crowd for his face, but Joe was again absent, I felt tormented, his brother-in-law was also absent that night, Francis sat in his usual space, ready to watch me sing, and the nightingale sang true that night, a song I had written myself.

I had many plans for my future with Joe. Escaping would be my biggest challenge. The lion's claws ran deep into my skin. I would not escape without injury, but Joe had other plans, sacrifice of the worst kind.

"I love you, Rose, you know that, please, just a little longer."

"I can't do this, Joe," I begged him, refusing to leave my quarters, I had done well in my recovery, the bottle remained full upon my dressing room table, but his persistence was an annoyance, I did not like being rushed. "I need to stay, just a little longer."

"You have three days. I will leave here, Rose. Willingly or otherwise you will come with me."

A scornful look hit my face. "You wish to save me?" I shook my head. He did not know the trauma I had faced before. The man claimed to want my hand. Fate tainted my hand. "I am a whore, Joe, and they will always see me as that. I have saved myself from the torment this world has. I will willingly come with you, but not before I have made peace with this world." I did not know his plan, but I feared it. "What have you planned, Joe, that has you so rushed?"

"They are willing to give a lot of money to those who catch the grave-robbers," he ambled towards me, holding my hands in his rough palms. "Rose, I can get that money, that's all we need to escape. I need you to ask Benjamin for your wage in trust. He holds it all from you, but you can request it whenever you wish."

"He won't..."

"Then threaten him, refuse to work, tell all those who pass your door of his deceitfulness, his greed, and he will soon pay."

"And what then, Joe? What happens when we have that but have nowhere we can go, the masons, to build our home, they are owned by the chambers, the farmers, who feed us, they are in their pockets, wherever we go they will find us, they're never going to let me go."

He wiped the tear from my face. A crushing pain deep in the pits of my stomach brought a sickness to me. I had dreamt of this moment, but now it was here. I feared nothing more.

"He will let you go, or I will die freeing you from this place, from your burden."

"Joe, I just need to know, why?"

"Because I love you, Rose, you're my Rose, the woman I heard so much about, and the moment I heard you sing, I knew, I knew from that moment I loved you."

Could I believe him, or would he be another, as soon as things became too difficult would he abandon me too, would he leave me by the side of a road to suffer, to be taken by the next, if we were to run out of food or shelter, would Joe be the one to find it, or would he be the one to fail me.

I had seen too much, I was too much, I was a singer, a whore, an addict, but worse still, I would always be spawn of the workhouse, destined to make mistake after mistake, I could never allow Joe to be a part of my world, I had to save him from myself, I was a lady once, but now, I was the product of a failing system.

"Evening, Rose," Benjamin stood by my door that evening, a smug look upon his face had me questioning.

"What brings you here?"

"News," he was playing with me, keeping the final reveal until I could take no more. "Of your..." Struggling for words, his lips began to pert, "Violation." He shook his head, not knowing the right word to use.

"What?" I burst towards him, a painful excitement filled my chest, my stomach twisted.

"Yes, a while ago, when in the care of one Thomas and Gladys Cartwright, you had a certain incident, which may have led you here, I believe it did anyway, to be taken so brutally at such a young age, so sad."

He saw my terrifying look of warning. "Tell me now."

"Fine, a man called Thomas Brack. They detained him this morning, for the rape of a young girl in the home of Gladys and Thomas Cartwright. The girl ran to the law, she didn't trust Gladys or Tom to do it for her, lucky for her, the man she spoke to was someone unrelated to their business, they had no choice but to arrest and sentence him, he will be on trial tomorrow."

"I don't know that name, Ben."

"No, but you may know him by face, he works closely alongside Thomas on one of the boats in the river, according to Thomas, he knew nothing about it," he leant towards me, a cruel look in his eyes shook me. "We all know he did,

Rose, it's what they do. They break you in before sending you off." I clenched my fists, feeling my fingernails digging into the palms of my hands. "They need to break you before they can control you, Rose. Surely you knew that?"

A bulging jaw warned him, I had no words for him, I had forgiven Gladys and Tom, I had let my hatred of them go completely only to feel it rushing back towards me, burning my stomach and heart, I did not want to hurt Gladys and Tom, I wanted them dead.

CHAPTER FIFTEEN WORKHOUSE RUINS

They had damaged me, the men of the Chambers, but they did not start this, they had taught me much, of instinct, 'twas not animalistic to hurt people, 'twas instinct, and normal, I am tainted, damaged goods, I knew this, but my life would never be complete, Joe had his plan, and now I had mine.

The workhouse taught forgiveness from the nuns, always told to forgive those who were less fortunate than ourselves, and yet, they would punish us for the crime of being a child, curious and innocent, they would beat us for the simplest of sins, something I wish to believe God would forgive me for. I made my mind up. I had received an unfair punishment, to bank my punishment for the crimes I had not yet committed. They would hurt no other.

"You want it all?" Ben raised his brows at me. I remained brave in the face of his annoyance.

"Every last bit of it."

"Why, Rose, you can't leave here, you know that; your wages are to keep you through your retired days."

"I do not plan to retire, besides," I drifted through the room, showing a confidence he had not born witness to before. "Do you believe I will ever leave here alive?"

He was silent for a moment. I tried to remain as calm as possible, 'twas my money he was holding from me. "Look, Rose, I would love to know why?"

He treaded softly. He did not wish to stir my anger, but he had no right to ask. "You may wish to know, but I will not discuss such investment with a man who is so parsimonious, it is my money to do with what I wish, the chambers were to keep it in trust until I decided, if you do not wish to return it, I can speak with Francis, I'm sure he knows many men of the law, or Jonathan for that matter, he too has connections with the law, after all, he is a sheriffs man, and one of my favourite clients, so, what will it be, Ben?"

"Give me an afternoon." His curling lip told me he felt defeated. My threats did not please him, but I was here for myself, and no one else.

I had planned to meet Joe in the town later that day, hoping to have my money secured by the evening. I would soon know his plan to escape.

"Is Isabelle not joining us?" I placed my arm over his. I did not care for the glares of callous hate from the ladies of the town. I was a lady, whether they liked it, being escorted by a proper gentleman. I knew their husbands, their brothers, and sons. If only they knew what I knew, they would not look down on me.

"Not today, she's resting. Last night we were lucky enough to return just on time." I quickly turned, knowing that a child had been born. "The family grows, their family at least. I only wish that I could one day have my own."

"Of course you can." I reached out, holding his face in my palm. "One day, Joe, you will have all you desire."

"And that's just you, Rose." Again, he meant for his sweet words to comfort me, but they made me doubt myself further. He was too good for me, he was everything to me, I should've felt more, but my heart did not race, my cheeks did not flush, I felt nothing but relief that soon this man would release me from my bonds, but at what cost to him.

"Joe, you can change your mind. We can be happy here..."

"Three days, just three days, Rose, and everything will change. We will be happy, and we will live our lives together. No one will ever know where we are..."

"And where do you plan on going?" I kept my voice quiet. The passing crowds could hear us, but they paid little attention to their busy lives.

"America," he was surely an idiot. "The lands are settling, the colonials, or France, Spain, will soon welcome us wherever you wish. We will have enough to escape this island and find a suitable home in Europe."

"Europe, I speak a little French, but not enough to live there."

"Then we will learn." His everlasting smile of hope concerned me. While his words were a romantic vision of what could be, he spoke as an idiot. He had not looked at the complications of such journeys.

"We are not rich, Joe."

"Not yet, but you will soon receive years of wages. That will surely be enough to get us away from Nottingham."

"My wages?" I mumbled, wondering what his plan was to increase our chances.

"Yes, and I have a plan as well. I can do this, but we have three days, Rose, and you need to be ready." His plan was flimsy at best. I could already see the holes. "In three days, I will wait for you at the side of your window with horse and carriage. I'll make it as late as I can, and after that, I promise we will escape."

"Joe, you don't seem to have thought this through."

"I have thought of every last detail, everything, Rose, we will be safe, you will be safe, I just need you to trust me, I will collect your wage tomorrow, whereupon I will see you two days from then, and we will escape."

He was a talker, but I was reluctant to hand anything over until I knew his plan in full.

"Just tell me your plan, Joe, everything."

His hesitation gave me little confidence until he burst. "The robbers, we have seen them at the graveyard, I know who they are and they plan on making a raid in three days, the body of John Corn is of great importance to them, so, I will follow them and catch them, after I collect my reward I will need a moment with my family, it will be the last I will see of them, Rose, after that I will come to you, there is a pipe leading from the side of your window, you can climb down that onto the carriage and we will make our way to the docks, a man called Grosvenor will meet us there, we can take his boat toward the east coast, when we reach Yarmouth there will be a ship waiting to take passengers to France, we can board for a few shillings, and when we reach France we will buy ourselves a horse and carriage and make our way toward the east, we will go as far as that horse can take us, the Lions Chambers has its fingers in many pies but China is not one of them, the exotics will see us fit for years of peace, there we can settle, knowing they will never find us, they will never know."

"It all sounds like a wonderful dream, Joe, and I can only wish 'twas possible, but I cannot see it. Perhaps the world has tainted my vision..."

"Then I will be your eyes. I will show you, prove to you exactly how kind the world can be. Trust me, Rose."

I did trust him. Upon the return to the chambers, I knew I would be busy that evening. Every Friday would be busy. The end of the working week would see my working weekend begin. I took my place within my quarters and performed as I always had, but my voice was dull, melancholy, my smile withered, I sang of the sorrowful winter to come, a winter of bare trees, hopes and dreams, I wanted to believe him, so I did.

I left my tincture in my quarters; I needed it; I needed my guide to show me my way, toward a desolate meadow, long dry grasses brushed my skin, a sound of children's laughter echoed along the empty plains, wind hissed through the trees and grasses, bliss hit my skin with the fresh beams of sun, I heard him call to me, my name echoed in the valleys. My trance broke to the glum reality I now faced, but something was not complete. I could not leave Nottingham knowing so many more would follow me. The chambers were a breeding ground for lies and deceit; the infection needed to end; I had to stop it, but I was only one person to face the mighty beast of the lions. I could not destroy the chambers, but I could have my revenge, I had less than two days to complete my task, I would end their stream of girls into the chambers, I would end Gladys and Tom, I did not know how, but I knew I had to, the tincture told me so.

Midnight struck. The bells of St Peters had haunted me since the day I had arrived. They were silent, the gifts I had accumulated over the years I packed, I had no interest in keeping them, but selling them was an option now, the fine jewels from Asia, the trinket boxes from Argentina, they would play a role in my freedom.

The streets were dark; I stepped towards my window, hoping to see a silent street. A watchman passed beneath my window, paying no heed to my presence above him. I quickened toward the balcony. Taking a cloak, I headed down the stairs.

The doorman, he saw me that night; I nodded to him, asking for a midnight walk. His concern was for my safety, but I promised him I would remain close to the lanterns. He believed my lies. Away from the chambers, I headed toward the shadows; I knew places such as Wool Street and Water Lane would offer more darkness than the main streets. Creeping my way towards Fisher Gate I felt my heart race, it had been so long since I had felt so alive, my blood rushing through my body, my every breath which left me brought danger to my whereabouts, but I was alive, and I would have my revenge.

Fisher Gate was wide. I would struggle for shadows, but I knew the place I needed to be, the place which would take me to the back of their home, New Street and into the courtyard. A poor lock upon their door saw me into the kitchen I knew so well, I removed the hood from my cloak, looking to that place, the place where it all went wrong, the moment in my life I had blamed for all too long, 'twas not my violation that began my poor fortune, 'twas them, they brought me here, they planned everything, forcing me into my addiction, forcing me to bare myself to the chambers, forcing me to hand over my life to them, I had rarely felt hate, but now I felt it rush through me.

The fish knife, sharp, it held secure in the palm; I took it in mine. With each step I took, I felt my heart shudder more, my stomach emptied from the hate I felt rushing into my arm.

I hated them both; they had taken everything from me. With the knife in hand, I crept toward their slumbering bodies. Tom, his face was a picture of protection once. A thick brown beard had now turned grey with age. His hair was now all but gone, and there she slept. My protector, Gladys, so peaceful in the dreams I would forever lock her in.

The knife was hard to pierce through skin. Fish and meat were much more tender than actual flesh, the screams soon dulled, I headed for the chest and neck; I knew little of the anatomy, but I knew how to butcher a pig, and that's what I was doing. They were filth, and they would never violate another girl again. The blood upon my ripped and torn hands was thick, the knife blade had broken in the chest of Tom just before he finished screaming, I knew to hit the heart, as much as I wanted them to suffer, seeing my face before their last breath was enough for me to feel my vengeance.

Rushing to the streets, a few lamps lit the houses inside. Scurrying as fast as I could from the back of the house I stumbled in the street, a bloody trail followed me, but luck was finally on my side, the heavens groaned, a small drop of rain landed in front of me as I knelt under darkened lamps.

The rain would be enough to wash away my sins from the street, but the thick blood remained sticky upon my hands. The canal was my only hope. Were I to be seen by anyone, covered with such an atrocity, I would lose my life. The water was icy on my skin; I washed all I could of my hands and face. A red stain would be enough to pass as overly stiff hands. The black cloak covered the blood on my clothes. I tried to walk, but knew I needed to rush. Hurrying back toward the chambers, the doorman awaited my arrival. As the door opened, Benjamin glared towards me from the shadow of the chambers bar.

"Where have you been? I came to pass you your wages you requested."

My breath was hard to catch. The rain had poured outside, bringing a smell to hide the stench of blood.

"Nowhere, I needed to clear my head is all."

"Your head has been clear since the moment you came here, Rose," he came closer, looking into my red and sore eyes. "Where have you been?"

His insistence forced me. "You will never have another innocent from them," I whispered. He furrowed his brow, not knowing what to say, what to think, or what to do. I held my stained hands towards him.

He grabbed my wrist, forcing my hand down; I checked over my shoulder, ensuring the doorman did not see. "What have you done?"

His hissing forced a twisted smile. A look of madness was befitting for my deed that night. "I took them off the books."

"Who?"

"You'll know, soon enough, you'll know."

Rushing towards my room I needed to clean myself, hoping Benjamin would understand that I was not as replaceable as he thought, I was the Rose of Nottingham, famed throughout the chambers of lions, they knew about me, and I was what kept the Nottingham chambers open, he had no power over me now, and he knew it.

"Someone tore them limb from limb..." I heard mumbling from the balcony. The sheriffs' men remained in the bar, speaking with Benjamin.

"Some of us thought it was probably an animal. The circus was at the docks recently, but no reports of missing bears. Then they saw the stab wounds."

"The killer is clearly deranged, their inners are now outers. The mess was horrific." I could see his stomach still churning. My work was something I was proud of, seeing their reaction to it. "Anyway, we are simply warning people, and asking if anyone saw anything?"

Benjamin turned; he saw me on the balcony. "Rose, you often sit by your window at night. Did you see a deranged bear pass by your window by chance?"

He did not lose his sarcasm on me. I could see the fear in his eyes. "No, nothing. Who is the victim?"

Benjamin looked so disappointed, something else I enjoyed seeing. "Gladys and Tom, sorry, Rose, I know you were close..."

"Not for a while now. The moment I came here, they didn't seem to care, so I left them to get on with their lives. 'Tis a shame though, I'll miss them at market."

I retired to my room, knowing I had piqued their interest. It was the first time I could remember feeling light without my vice. I had killed, I was a murderer, and I was proud of it.

The town was a hive of activity that morning. I headed towards the market, knowing I would need to be back before my time upon the stage. I loved hearing their tales, chatting on the streets of the monster that had torn the fishmongers apart in the night.

"They found some intestine in the street, said it was definitely an animal..."

The whispers were the thing of nightmares. "Jonathan," I called as I passed by him. He was on duty. I knew I needed to tread lightly. I did not want him to suspect me.

"Morning, Rose."

"Morning, I heard about last night," I walked beside him through the busy market, "it's worrying."

"Very worrying, but what's worse is this was a person, someone we believe to be quite small as well."

"Do you have any leads?" I pressed him but he was reluctant to answer, "You know I was close to Gladys and Tom."

"I know, but we have nothing, they're looking but doubt they'll find them, Rose. These things are so hard to solve." He looked at my satin gloves. "You're bleeding, Rose, are you alright?"

"I'm fine. Argument with a mirror is all. It rather upset me to hear of Gladys and Tom. I'm rather absent minded at the moment."

"Understandable," he stopped walking and turned toward me, "Don't listen to them, Rose, all these people think they know what happened, but they know nothing, we will do our best to find the person who did this, Rose, but don't listen to ill-formed rumours, just keep doing your best, hold your head up, and you'll be fine."

"Officer..." a dishevelled man called out, stood at the side of Jonathan and I. "Do you think this is the same bloke who killed all those prostitutes?"

Jonathan was unnerved as he looked at me. "It's fine."

"We have the culprit responsible for those attacks. This one was different. A top investigator from London will join us this afternoon. We believe it was something more personal." I felt my blood run cold, tiny hairs on my arm stood on end.

"Personal?" asked the gent who thought hard about their dealing in the town. "Well, nothing more personal than feeling abandoned by them." He raised his brow to Jonathan, who paid attention to the man's words. "All I'm saying is, I'm a smith myself, I have apprentice after apprentice, learning the trade and following my hands, had four in my time, but Gladys and Tom, a new one each year," his eyes drifted about the crowd attempting to insert an idea of mystery. "No one has that many girls coming through their home without seeing a resentment. I ain't clever, but you don't need no high-brow investigator to tell you, you need to be looking into those girls."

"If you saw the bodies, Mark, you would know it was no woman who did that, certainly no ruin of a workhouse." Jonathan looked at me. He did not mean for talk of such vulgarity to be heard by a lady. "'Twas a man or monster who inflicted those wounds, Mark. It would help us more if they limited the search to what we know, not what we assume."

It weakened me with sickness, the people knew, but the sheriffs' men refused to think of a woman having such dominant power. The chambers were quiet as I returned, glaring eyes met me from a table in the corner of the bar, Benjamin sat with a glass in hand, dishevelled, I knew it was not his only glass of the morn, his head wobbled in a drunken state as he looked towards me.

His eyes invited me to sit with him, 'twas not a place for a woman or lady, but my manager insisted I sit and so I did.

Silence broke as his clouded eyes looked at me, the sweat on his brow dampened his hair.

"You don't look well." I mentioned to him in his drunken state.

He took a swig from his glass, "I went somewhere this morning, to see the result of what animals do when let off their leash."

I raised my head and straightened my back. "Anger, Ben, 'tis a dangerous thing, especially when they do not explore that anger."

"Have you taken your vice today?" his scowl burnt towards me.

"I have no need of it yet, you?"

"You know I don't partake in that stuff," he sneered, his fear clouded his anger. "Why did you do it, Rose?" I did not reply. I enjoyed his fear of me, his wondering if I could deliver the same fate to him. "They did nothing. They brought you here, to me, Rose, to the place that made you who you are today."

"That's right, they did, when I came here, I was nothing but an innocent child, a child of misfortune, they taught me their trade and I was grateful for that, what I was not grateful for was being raped by a friend of Tom, set to the lions by Gladys, and turned into your singing whore, they come every night to the chambers to hear me sing, and violate me further." I felt a maddened wildness within my eyes, stretching towards him. I looked through him. He was not worthy of my vision. "I came here wanting to become a lady of the town, respected and wanted, by a real gentleman, even the devil wouldn't have me now, it all started there, Ben, it all started with the violation of my body, caused by them, I am no monster for what I did, they are, I simply showed their truth to the world, I know I was not the first girl Gladys and Tom had defiled," I leant closer to him taking the warm glass he clutched in his fist, "but I will be the last, the lions will hurt no other, no more Billy's, no more Roses, get your house in order, Ben, you've seen what I can do, nothing makes you special, I will willingly do the same to all those who pass through these doors and you cannot stop me." His eyes widened; he had lost his power.

"Because without me, this place would close, you would have nothing without me, Ben, there is only one Rose of Nottingham, and the rose has thorns, be weary of what you do next, turn me in and I will see this place in ashes by the end of the night, I own you, Ben, I own all those here, they love me, they revere me, and they would do anything I ask of them."

He could not reply as I stood, I took a slow walk back to my chambers, running my fingers across the gilded bar as I did, I felt the wood of the banister, the gold opulence of the lions upon the newel, heavy wood was sturdy beneath my feet as I glided up the stairs, I had never stood so proud, knowing; it was all mine.

The world had changed, 'twas now in my favour, as the evening lingered as did I, I held my head low, knowing what I had done, I was almost free from that godforsaken town, I only needed to survive one more day. Joe would arrive with his horse and carriage, ready to whisk me away to a brighter future. I took my place upon the stage, gave them an hour of enjoyment before finally retiring. I had many planned that evening to visit me, but I remained distant from them. Every thought entered my mind. Could I escape such a heinous deed? Would Joe still love me if he knew what I had done? I infatuated the man, but I was not with him.

The evening saw Jonathan at my door. He had not planned to see me that evening, but given the recent events, 'twas no surprise he had come knocking. I felt his eyes upon me as he stood proudly in my room. I slumped before him, withering like a dying rose.

"I assume the reality has now hit?" he asked, believing he knew the reason for my depressive state.

"It is slowly hitting; it makes me wonder though." I needed to test him. I needed to check that his knowledge of the crime did not run so deep. "Although I'm sure they had their enemies, who would do such a thing to another human?"

His lip curled, "A monster, Rose, you needn't worry, I believe we may have caught the culprit, some of the locals pointed to a travellers' camp on the side of the Leen, we believe one of those to be responsible." I felt my stomach twist. I may have committed those crimes against Gladys and Tom, but to see an innocent fall for my crime was beyond what I could cope with. "Anyway, how is that hand?"

He leant forward, inspecting my gloved hands. I had cut both, but he had only seen one bleed.

"I'm fine," I gave a wide smile, noticing him turn his head toward the mirror on my dressing table.

Pointing towards it, I could tell he was struggling to speak. He dare not accuse me of such heinous crimes. "I thought you said something broke it?"

"It was, Jonathan. We are in the Lion's Chambers, where nothing remains broken for long." I relaxed my smile to him, creating a comfort from his suspicion.

"Ah," he lifted his head, "well, just keep your windows closed at night. I shudder to think what would happen if something happened to you." A brief grin from the corner of his mouth warmed me as he turned. "Our Rose of Nottingham, where would we be without you?"

"I shall take that as a rhetorical question." I saw him to the door, knowing I had paled all suspicions he was carrying. I had no fear now. Even if he knew I was responsible, he would struggle to see me from these walls.

The morning brought a light summer rain. The fresh smell of the drops of water drifted into my window, the sound of hissing puddles as the carriages passed by shushed me in my waking. The rain comforted me that day, it spoke to my mood, some would see the rain as a misery, a day ruined, I saw it as a chance to wash away my sins, I would not dance in the rain, but simply watching the tiny drops run down my window was enough.

A sound in the chambers below caught my attention. I would remain indoors that day and await my saviour in the night, but the arguing drew me away from my window.

"Are you sure?" I heard a call.

"I am surer than any. I have someone who is inside the operation who will help." Percy, a sweaty little man of no reputation whatsoever, had joined Francis in the lower chambers.

Peering from my door, I saw Francis's eyes drift toward my door. I paid no attention to him. "I would help you, Percy, but I need to know you are sure," he darted towards him, angered, "you know what this would mean for the chambers if you are correct, our entire board will need to know of this."

"He has been helping them for years. This is probably how he funds his stay at the chambers, as well as the nice new house they have." His hissing and spitting noted he clearly spoke of someone he despised.

"Percy, you keep this completely silent, if this is correct, be mindful he has a new child, and two others, a wife who dotes on him, the entire community love him, even if he causes most of their deaths within the town." I was no fool. I could not work out who they spoke of.

"Well, I know someone who can help, all I ask is that you are ready yourself, I know how close you are to him," his voice spoke of sympathy, "but from this evening, he will no longer be a burden to this town."

Storming from the chambers I saw Francis age a decade before me, if only I had known the blow they had delivered to him, but I did not know who Percy spoke of, I had seen Percy in and out of the chambers, he had never visited me, he paid no attention to my voice when on the stage, there was only one other like that, George Smith, a man I had never spoken to.

The evening came and went, Joseph, with all his infatuation, arrived below my window, the night was still, 'twas wet and cold, a brisk breeze ran through my blood, I froze with terror, but I knew it was now or never, a small bag of clothes would be enough to see us to our new lives together, I did not love Joe, but in time I believed I could.

The door burst open. "Rose, is this true?" Benjamin stood, shaken at the door. I looked to the street below, ready to jump from the window, hoping the carriage would break my fall. "Rose!" he bellowed toward me; I did not know what he was speaking of.

Jonathan stood behind him, as did Francis. "What is all this?" I moused out with a raspy voice; they knew.

"Rose, if you have done something, we can help you," said Francis. Benjamin burst in.

Grabbing my wrists, he pulled my gloves off. "What did you do, Rose?"

"Nothing," I quivered, fearing for my life I could think of only one thing I could do.

"The chambers are falling apart, first George and now this," grumbled Francis.

"George?"

"They found George Smith aiding and abetting the escape of convicts, turned in by his own brother-in-law." I shook my head.

Looking to the ground, I heard myself mumble. 'No.'

"And then this, we discover you murdered your former employers..."

"No!" I screamed, forcing myself free from Benjamin's grasp. "George did not save criminals."

"She's clearly insane, I told you, that is what opium does..." Jonathan burst, my eyes drifted to the street below. How could he? How could he accuse his own family of such crimes? I know the reward would see us well, but it was not worth the life of George Smith.

"He did it!" my screams echoed to the streets below, "I was there, I took the knife from his hands, but I did not hurt them, I only wanted him to scare them, for them to know what they did to me, I never wanted them dead, but he did." I begged Francis with the eyes I knew he could not refuse, "Uncle, you believe me, don't you?"

Benjamin knew, he knew Joseph was innocent, but he was pitiful. He would not argue.

"Rose, do not speak of that again, Jonathan, go," ordered Francis in a deep, drilling voice. They stormed from the room, where I watched. I watched my only chance of freedom being led down the street to face punishment for a crime I had committed. I would never be free. I was a lady once, but now, I was nothing but a whore. The Lions Chambers Gentleman's Club was not only my home, 'twas my stage, it was my new vice.

THE END.

A Brief History of Nottingham

Nottingham in the early 1800s, although portrayed here as being rather dark and gloomy, would've been a vastly different place indeed. It wasn't until the late 19th century that Nottingham managed to hit city status by the charter of Queen Victoria.

The notable buildings surrounding Nottingham prove that a distinct plan was in the works from the mid-1800s until they realised the status. With many of the buildings containing dated stones, it is clear that a huge campaign of building occurred during this time, industry was always at the forefront of Nottingham's growth, the infrastructure of the city shows that great care was taken to include its major industrial growth such as textiles, which specialised in lace, coal was also a major industry which was helped by the opening of the canals in Nottingham.

WORKHOUSES

The Sutton workhouse opened in around 1770. The workhouse was not only a place for the poor, unfortunate, and orphaned, or abandoned children, it appears it was also a place of meetings.

The books of the Workhouse Accounts have disappeared, and the Minutes in the Vestry books alone remain to give any information concerning its management. On the 23rd of April 1781, they appointed John Boler of Mansfield Woodhouse to overlook the poor at the Public Workhouse at Sutton-in-Ashfield for three months.

On the 23rd of February 1790, Saml. Wilson and his wife of H. Huthwaite were appointed Overseers of the Workhouse.

In 1791 at the meeting previously alluded to Hardwick Close was let towards building the new Workhouse, and on the 20th of May 1795, at a meeting at the house of Ralph Wass, it was agreed that in the future, parish business be transacted in the Vestry of the Parish Church.

On the 1st of November 1796, Saml Wilson was hired to look after the Workhouse, and was no doubt the surgeon and apothecary before alluded to, and we may imagine that this curt and undignified entry was due to his requiring an advance of salary, while it forms an interesting comparison with the status and salary of the medical men of today. He, however, did not keep it long.

On the 23rd of May 1797, Joseph Parkin and Elizabeth, his wife, were appointed to the office. No record appears of the number of inmates, nor of their lodging, feeding or length of residence.

At a Vestry meeting at Church on the 24th of February 1800, Thomas Dove and his wife were appointed Master and Mistress of the Workhouse and to have maintenance for

himself, wife and two smallest children, and for an encouragement to promote industry in the said Workhouse he shall have one penny out of every shilling that is earned in the Workhouse. This entry reminds us of the fact that persons were provided with work in the Workhouse, and stocking frames were the usual means employed at Sutton. Indeed, as late as 1860 stocking frames were used at the House of Correction at Southwell.

OPIUM TRADE IN THE 1800S

"There were opium dens where one could buy oblivion, dens of horror where the memory of old sins could be destroyed by the madness of sins that were new." Oscar Wilde in his novel, 'The Picture of Dorian Gray' (1891).

The largely unregulated pharmaceutical trade throughout history has led to many discoveries that would today have us calling our local councillor, or even news broadcaster, while a strange practice today, in the 1800s, medicine such as sleeping medications for children, cough and cold cures, would often contain opiates, alcohol, and even mercury.

Laudanum and Godfrey's Cordial was used mostly on children as a sleeping aide, poorer families would purchase Godfrey's cordial to allow the mother to obtain work, allowing the child to sleep while the mother worked ensured her income, which they would often heavily rely on.

Laudanum addicts would enjoy highs of euphoria followed by deep lows of depression, along with slurred speech and restlessness. Withdrawal symptoms included aches and cramps, nausea, vomiting and diarrhoea, but even so, it was not until the early 20th century that it was officially recognised as addictive.

Although the drug has its historical ties, it is not outdated, still active to this day. The opioid epidemic claims 91 American lives each day, according to the Centres for Disease Control and Prevention. It's the deadliest drug epidemic in history, thanks to the potency and the type of drugs involved. But the epidemic today parallels the laudanum and morphine overuse outbreak of the late 1800s in many important ways, even sharing some of the same causes and racial disparities — and perhaps offering lessons on how to rein in addiction.

PROSTITUTION AND DRUG USE

It is often claimed that prostitution is the oldest trade in the world. While this may be true, it comes with the cruelty of exploitation and drug use. Many countries suffer at the hands of those who wish to exploit both men and women for their own monetary gain.

Throughout history, women have had to sell themselves to feed their families, as well as addictions, such as drugs and alcohol, but it isn't all sinister, in many countries, prostitution is now being looked upon as a legitimate trade, as well as a form of entertainment, taking a step back in time to the Roman Empire, one of notable strength, their exploiting of men and women was revered and often slaves within their masters homes would ask to be placed into such trade, knowing they would be better fed and cared for, it was also classed as an enjoyable career.

While frowned upon today, this was because of the subject of sex becoming a huge taboo subject during a time when church was heavily involved in both the personal and political lives of the people of their parish. However, times do change, as we look upon prostitution today as a somewhat off-putting trade. Many countries are now open to the idea of reopening brothels.

The sex industry was worth over £184 Billion worldwide. A figure I struggle to comprehend. Figures compiled from Havoscope 2021.

CRIMES AGAINST WOMEN

Throughout history, women seem to have drawn the short straw, although we would like to think we have moved with the times. The truth is that women are still undervalued in many areas and countries. It was in the 1800s that this began to change, gradually, but still a change was apparent. Crimes against women, such as rape and battery, were punishable by death. In fact, there are several entries in historical law where rapists have been placed to the gallows. Battery would receive a lesser sentence, but a sentence, nonetheless.

The evidentiary practice has changed throughout history, while in the 1800s an accusation would be viewed as evidence, this is no longer the case, with the progression of technology such as fingerprinting, DNA extraction and doctors who specialise in domestic abuse and violence, women are now more protected than ever.

In the year ending March 2019, 1.6 million women experienced domestic abuse, 2 women each week are killed by their partners, these figures are from the UK alone, which opens our eyes to the fact that in such a safe and stable society, violence against women is still very real and an issue we must always talk about. The unfairness of society has still not ended and no man or woman should stop until it has ended completely.

THE NOTTINGHAM COCKLE MAN

Whilst they have documented the cockle man of Nottingham and many cities throughout history as an honest trade, I would like to take the chance to dedicate this to Dave Bartram, the last cockle man of Nottingham.

Dave has served the community of Nottingham City Centre for over 50 years, as odd  as it may seem to some from other cities and even countries, it was a standard practice on a Saturday night out to see Dave within the pubs and clubs of Nottingham serving his prawns, cockles, mussels and occasional pepperami™ stick. He is instantly recognisable to those of Nottingham, clad in his white uniform upon an evening and a pleasure to talk to.

A very modest man, we hailed Dave as a legend in Nottingham, as he desperately tried to keep his ancient trade alive. The cockle man is held in such high esteem in Nottingham that he even has his own parody Twitter account - usually the reserve of national celebrities - and over 1,600 people have joined a Facebook campaign, calling for him to be given the Freedom of the City. In

2019, Nottingham City Transport named a number 10, Ruddington, bus after Mr Bartram, to honour his great service to the city.

In 2021, during the time The Rose of Nottingham was being written, Dave Bartram still had no plans to retire. It is doubtful he ever will.

ACKNOWLEDGEMENTS

Mr Bartram, our legend of Nottingham, who still provides cockles to this day despite being over 60 miles from the sea. Your service to Nottingham has never gone unnoticed.

My husband, Phill, who tries his best daily to keep the kids entertained, allowing me time to write.

The three kids, Rubie, Lylah and Kal-El, once again, without you I would be on my 70th novel by now. Cheers kids!

Printed in Great Britain
by Amazon